Freak Camp

*Posts From a Previously
Normal Girl*

Jessica V. Barnett

Second edition, published in 2017.

Copyright © 2017, 2014 Jessica V. Barnett

Cover design and back photograph by Brent M. Hale.

Cover photograph by Patrick Barnett-Mulligan.

Map by Peter M. Barnett

Available at Amazon.com and other online stores.

ISBN-10: 0692939563
ISBN-13: 978-0692939567

Also by Jessica V. Barnett

Girlflight (Freak Camp, Vol. 2)

The Queen of Sheba: a novella

For Hayden, Casey, Otis, and Felix,

with love

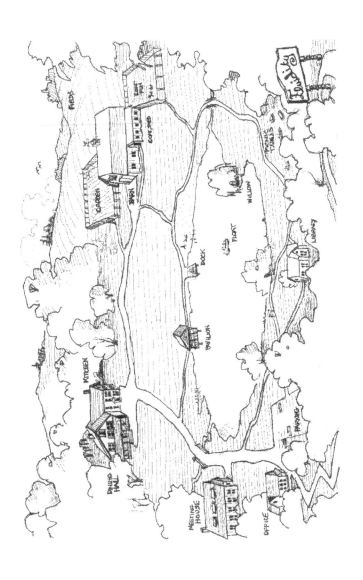

Map of the Fluidity Campus

1

Tonight we are having "dinner for six." That's what my mom calls it when she and my stepmom, my sister and I, and my two stepbrothers are all together for dinner at our house in Darwin. A better name for it would be "feeding time at the zoo." If Layla and I were at our dad's apartment in the city, I'd probably be eating takeout sushi and sipping sparkling water out of a martini glass. Instead, I'm eating spaghetti and hot dogs (the only thing that my younger stepbrother, Matty, will eat right now) and stressing out about which high school I'm going to visit tomorrow.

There are four high schools in Darwin because there are four kinds of people. I mean, there are all kinds of people, but there are four sources of people: Earth, Air, Water, and Fire. When you're young, you don't have to know which one you are. People usually grow into their source around ten or eleven years old.

I'm thirteen, and I still don't know what I am.

With some people, like my sister, Layla, it's obvious. She's a Water. One look at her eyes, and you would know that. They have this "stormy sea" quality that other people can't shut up about. Annoying. Plus, there's the fact that ever since she was eight, she sprouts gills and fins when she's in saltwater. That was kind of a dead giveaway.

I hope that I'm an Earth, like my mom. She is so beautiful. Her body gives off this warm glow, and when she walks by the plants and flowers in the yard they lean into her, as if she were the sun, making them grow.

My fourteenth birthday is coming up in August, and if I don't identify by then, I swear I'll die.

No, really.

Because when you're fourteen, you're supposed to start source school with the other people in your group. My sister started Darwin Water School two years ago. She's always going on about her favorite class, Techniques in Underwater Breathing. Like she's so hot because she can stay underwater for hours at a time. Prancing around the house in her blue DWS jacket.

Annoying.

Then there's my stepbrother, Devon. He's only five, and he already knows what he is. Well, with Devon it's not really fair, because he's a Fire. It's a little hard to miss when he gets excited, and blue flames start to flare up on his fingertips. Not to mention, whenever he meets someone, before they even ask him, he says, "I'm Devon. I'm five. I'm a Fire."

Annoying.

Anyway, girls are practically never Fire. Thank God. Who wants to sleep on those scratchy flame-retardant sheets your whole life anyway? No, thanks.

"I think you should come to DWS," says Layla.

Big surprise.

"I've seen DWS a million times," I say. "I feel like I am there every other day to watch you swim. Besides, don't you think my gills would have come out by now? … I'm thinking of going to DES."

"You just want to hang out with May," says Layla.

May is my best friend from school. She identified as an Earth last fall. I don't see her as much now because she goes to Earth classes at DES in the afternoons. But we're still best friends … at least for now. Next year, she'll be at DES full time. If I end up there, we can stay best friends, and nothing will have to change. Please, God!

"What about DAS?" Airhead butts in. Airhead is my stepmom. She's an Air. Her real name is Jackie. She and the boys moved in with us last year after she and my mom got married. Whatever.

"What a great idea," says my mom. "You've never been to DAS before."

"Mom, there's a reason I've never been there. Because no one in our family is an Air, so why would I go?" Airhead's lips go tight. My mom frowns.

"You know what I mean," I say. "No one that I'm related to." I can see that I am just making things worse, so I switch topics. "What about DFS? I've never been there before either."

Devon shrieks with laughter. "You can't go to Fire school. That's for boys!"

"Who says?"

"Everybody knows that, stupid." He shoots a fireball past my face for good measure.

"Devon, language!" yells Airhead. "One more fireball and you're in time out!"

Airhead gets up from the table to get some more milk for Matty.

As soon as she turns her back, Devon sends another fireball flying across the table at me. My mom's about to say something to him when Matty reaches out from his seat and grabs the fireball with his bare hand. Airhead sees it and flips out.

"Matty, no! Devon, TIME OUT! Get in your room!" A big gust of air slams the refrigerator door shut, and all the papers on the countertop fly up and scatter around the room. Typical Airhead. She runs over to the table, yelling, "Matty, are you okay? Open your hand!"

Then it happens. The fireball just fizzles out with this "pop," and water sprays out from Matty's fist, right into his face. He starts laughing like it's the funniest thing that's ever happened to him. Then Airhead is laughing, and my mom, and Layla. Everyone gathers around Matty, telling him how lucky he is to identify at three years old, and Layla's acting like he's her special pet because he's a Water, too.

Plus, no one even remembers that Devon is supposed to be in time out.

Now we know Matty is a Water, and I'm the only unidentified one left. That's it. Tomorrow is the last day of school, and I'm making it my mission this summer to find out my source. There is no way I'm going to that lame private school for unidentifieds. No way.

2

I wake up after 7:00 the next morning, with my head at the foot of the bed and all my covers in a pile on the floor. Guess I was a little restless. I throw on shorts and a tee shirt and hightail it downstairs, but I'm still the last one down to breakfast. I hate that.

"Mom, I told you to wake me up at 6:30!"

"Good morning to you, too, Celeste. I'm sorry, I forgot to wake you, sweetie. I brought Layla to practice this morning, and I was a little late getting back. Are you hungry?"

I sit down at my seat, where a plate of cold eggs is staring me in the face. "No thanks," I say.

"I'm glad you're here," Airhead chimes in. "We have an announcement we want to make."

This should be interesting.

"What about Layla? She should be here." I protest.

My mom says, "I know, sweetie, but this one was just too good to wait. I told Layla on her way to practice this morning."

"And that, actually, is the reason for this announcement," says Airhead. "Your mom and I have been talking for some time about how to ease the burden of all these morning practices. We also know how much all you kids love to swim. And now, with Matty being a Water, it won't be so dangerous for him, so … we thought it was about time to get a pool in our backyard!"

Mom says, "And this way, I won't have to drive Layla to the Ocean Center every morning."

Yes, finally, a pool!

Then it starts to dawn on me …

"Wait a minute," I say. "We're getting a *saltwater* pool?"

"Of course," she says. "That way Layla can do her fin practice at home, and when Matty gets older—"

I don't wait around to hear the rest. I just bolt back up to my room and shut the door. *Saltwater?* Just because Layla's a Water and Matty's a Water, we all have to swim in saltwater?

My mom and Airhead knock on the door. Mom asks, "Celeste, may we come in?"

"Not her. Just you."

I can hear Airhead's footsteps retreating down the hall. Mom comes in and sits next to me on the bed. Rover, the potted plant on my side table, bends his leaves around to touch her on the arm. She brushes them gently away.

"Sweetie, are you okay? I don't understand. I thought you wanted a pool."

"I said I wanted a regular pool. Saltwater is disgusting. It stings."

"But the ocean is saltwater. You love to swim at the beach."

"That's not the same."

"Well, I'm sorry, but the decision's been made. I can't keep driving Layla to the Ocean Center every morning. I thought you'd be happy. Now I'll be here to make you breakfast. ... Celeste?"

"What?"

"I know it's hard."

"What?"

"Identifying so late. I mean, I didn't identify until I was fourteen, you know that. Even then I wasn't really sure. But back then, there was no choice. They didn't have mixed schools. There are so many more options today. Fluidity is a great private school, and it's right here—"

"I am NOT going to that hippie school for unidentified freaks!"

"There's nothing wrong with—"

"I'm NOT! I'd rather die!"

"Celeste!"

Her eyes fill with tears, which makes me want to cry, too. Rover starts to droop.

"I'm sorry," I say. "I didn't mean it. Can you just leave me alone, please? I have to get ready for school."

"Okay," she says. "But we're going to talk about this more later. It's serious when you talk that way."

"Fine," I say, and she leaves the room. Ugh. Another great start to the day.

I look in the mirror. My eyes are blue, like Layla's, but flat. No stormy seas here. My dark blonde hair extends down, limp and lifeless, to a couple of inches below my shoulders. The only standouts here are the two fantastically dark freckles on the tip of my nose. Well, at least it's the last day of school.

There's something to be excited about.

The middle school and the elementary school are down the street from each other, both within walking distance of our house. Layla takes the bus to DWS, or my mom drives her if she has an early morning practice—which is always—and Airhead drops Matty at preschool on her way to work. That means I have to walk Devon to kindergarten every day.

Today, when we walk out the front door, Devon sees his friend at the corner and bolts down the hill, leaving me in the dust. As I run to catch up, I can feel the sweat soak through my tee shirt under the straps of my backpack. Great.

After I drop Devon off, I walk down the street and loiter a bit outside the middle school, trying to air dry my armpits. The school is a big brick rectangle, with strips of metal-framed windows on each floor. The kid factory, we call it, because of its assembly-line classrooms, evenly spaced along endless hallways lined with graying subway tile and rusting green lockers.

By the time I get inside, May is already there, putting her lunch in her locker. She's wearing a lime green tank top with "Every Day is Earth Day" written across the front. No armpit stains there. She is flawless. As she turns around to greet me, a few light brown curls escape from her signature May ponytail.

"Hey," I say.

"Hey."

"You won't believe what happened this morning. First, I found out we're getting a pool this summer, and I'm thinking, great! And then they tell me it's gonna be saltwater, which is like, disgusting. I am never swimming in that thing. We should just keep swimming at the town pool—"

"CJ?" May calls me that because my last name is Jardine.

"Yeah?"

"My mom told me this morning, she signed me up for camp."

"I know, but it's only half days. We can go to the pool in the afternoons."

"No, not Medley Camp. She signed me up for overnight source camp. Eight weeks. I leave this weekend."

"Source camp, already? I thought you were going to be at Medley this summer."

"I thought I was too, it's just, my mom thought I'd be better prepared for school next fall if I went to Earth camp, and then I got into Gray Rock."

"Gray Rock? That's like three hours away. Are you okay with that?"

"Yeah. Sort of. I mean, it's a great camp. My brother is a counselor there."

The bell rings, and we hustle down the hall to homeroom. No May this summer? What next?

3

At 10:00 a.m., we're busy scrubbing the tables in the physics lab—isn't there some kind of law against child labor?—when someone comes in and hands a note to the teacher. That's hardly ever a good sign. The teacher looks up ... directly at me.

"Celeste, Ms. Fairfax needs to see you."

I shoot May a look of panic. She looks back at me and winces.

"Right now?" I say.

"Yes. Please go down to her office. It shouldn't take long."

Ms. Fairfax is the school guidance counselor. I guess I've been avoiding her. She wants all the eighth graders to fill out pre-registration forms for source school next year. For obvious reasons, I haven't gotten around to it yet.

Ms. Fairfax's "office" is basically a closet next to the cafeteria, with just enough room for a desk (really, just a table), two chairs, and a filing cabinet. The door is open when I get there. Ms. Fairfax is sitting behind the desk. She seems to have taken her role as "jaded middle school guidance counselor" to heart because she is wearing a shin-length khaki skirt, a blouse with a collar that ties into a bow, and a saggy blue cardigan. I'm also ninety percent sure that she is wearing knee-highs. Oh, Ms. Fairfax, what happened to you?

"Ms. Swergold-Jardine, please come in," she says, when she sees me in the doorway.

"It's just Jardine," I say. "Swergold is my middle name."

At my age, someone calling you by your last name usually precedes some kind of punishment. Can a guidance counselor hold you back for not turning in your year-end paperwork? I'm not sure.

I sit down and prepare for the worst.

"They told me to come and see you?" I say. For some reason, it comes out as a question.

"Yes. It's the last day of school."

Tell me something I don't know.

She goes on, "so I am meeting with all the eighth-grade students who have not turned in their source school pre-registration paperwork. Did you see the forms in your mailbox? It's very important that we get an early start on this, so the high schools can begin their planning process."

"Yes, I did. I meant to do it—"

"Well, there's no time like the present. Let's just get through this quickly, so we can cross you off. It's really very painless ... okay, so, we'll need to put down a source group for you."

Painless, right. Painless like a trip to the dentist.

I say, "You know, I think I filled this out already. I just left it at home—"

11

She taps her pen on the paper, until I get the message and stop talking. She forces a smile and says, "Well, at this point, we might as well do it while you're here. You are a Water, I believe?" She jots down "W" on the form without even looking at me.

"No, that's my sister."

"Oh, of course. How is Layla? The most beautiful eyes. Is she enjoying DWS?"

"I think so."

"Okay, then, what is your source, dear? Or shall we put a 'U' for now? We need to put something."

She crosses out the "W" and looks up at me, expectantly.

This torture has to stop.

I look around the room, desperate for an escape plan, but all she has on her desk is a nameplate, a couple stacks of paper, and a half-empty coffee mug with a picture of Mount Rushmore on it. Desperate times call for desperate measures. For her sake, I hope that the coffee has had time to cool.

I lean forward, "Is that Mount Rushmore on your mug? I've always wanted to go there." My hand bumps the mug—accidentally, of course—and it tips toward her, splashing coffee onto the front of her blouse and creating a stream across the table straight into her lap. Luckily, it feels cool to the touch.

"Oh, my word!" she says.

My word? Do people really say that anymore? Okay. Focus.

"I am SO sorry," I say. I grab some paper from the stack nearest to me and start using it to blot up the coffee stream.

"No! No. Please don't! That's all right." She grabs the wet papers from my hands.

"Do you want me to get some paper towels from the girls' bathroom?" I offer.

"No, no, I'll take care of it. Just, please, bring this home with you, and tell your mother she needs to return it by the end of the week, or there will be no one in the office to process it."

"Absolutely. I will let her know how important this is."

"Oh, and make sure you sign up for one of the high school trips this afternoon. The lists are posted outside the door."

"No problem. Sure." I back out the door. Out in the hall, I scrawl my name on the list for DES and look down at the coffee-stained form in my hands. "Name: Celeste Swergold Jardine. Source: blank." That about sums it up.

I rip the paper in half and throw it into the trash can on the way back to class.

4

After lunch, the entire eighth grade gathers by the front doors of the school to board the buses for source school orientation. I stick with May and the Earth crew, a pretty diverse mix of boys and girls, tall and short, fat and thin. Easy to blend in.

Glancing over at the Waters, I'm thankful I decided not to go to DWS this afternoon. The Water girls are all at least half a foot taller than me. They are muscular, lean, Amazon warriors, toned from hours of laps in the pool. The Water boys are lean and muscular, too. They are a pretty good-looking group. But according to Layla, most Water boys are more into each other than they are into girls. That could explain why the Water girls are so busy trying to get the attention of the Fire guys.

The Fire guys are, um, interesting-looking. I count at least ten Mohawks out of a group of maybe thirty-five guys. That's almost a third. Pretty impressive statistics. Not to mention at least half of them have body art, or at least one piercing. Well, they say opposites attract. They are all yours, Water girls.

Looking over at the Airs, nothing much stands out about them. By looks alone, you wouldn't really be able to tell them from the Earths. But there is something about them. They seem to like to shout at each other. They talk louder, laugh louder … they are more in-your-face than the Earths. Like Fires, but without the flames.

A smaller, fifth group is gathered next to the Airs. The NPs. NP is for New Preston, the city where my dad lives, about a forty-minute drive from Darwin. The NP kids get bused in to Darwin from the city every day.

"What are they doing over there?" I ask May. "Aren't they coming?"

"What for?" says May. "They aren't going to high school here. Busing stops after middle school."

"Oh, yeah."

We board the bus for DES and make the short drive across town. Like all the public schools in Darwin, the outside of the building is unremarkable. Just another big brick kid factory.

But when we get inside, my mouth drops open. I can see that the two-story brick building wraps around a giant greenhouse the size of a football field. On the outside wall, the corridors look just like the middle school, with the faded tile and rows of rusty lockers. But the inside walls are glass, giving an unobstructed view of the courtyard gardens.

I listen for the familiar hum of bad fluorescent lighting. Nothing. All the lights in the hallways are off. Instead, sunlight streams in through the glass. I suddenly realize that I'm uncomfortably warm. I quickly take off my backpack to avoid a repeat of this morning's sweat stains.

I survey the greenhouse. Row after row of planting beds overflow with flowers and vegetables, some familiar and some that I have never seen before. I spot a purple pumpkin. A row of vines with grapes the size of kiwis. A group of students tends to one of the nearby beds, laughing and talking as they toss weeds into a wheelbarrow. I imagine myself and May as part of that group, chatting and sunning ourselves while we work.

A man's voice snaps me out of my daydream.

"Welcome, students. My name is Mr. Drake. I'm the vice-principal here at DES. Every year, we like to give our incoming class a sneak peek behind our walls to see what's in store for the fall. Of course, some of you have been coming here for advanced coursework this spring, so you have a bit of a head start. Right, Ms. Jacobs?"

The vice-principal beams at May, and everyone turns in our direction. May flashes her winning smile, while I blush like an idiot. It doesn't matter, I tell myself. They are all looking at her anyway.

Mr. Drake introduces a group of DES students who have volunteered to show us around for the afternoon. May and I stick together as they divide us up into groups of four or five. Our group heads down the hall to one of the botany labs. My hopes of chatting with May all afternoon out in the sun are quickly crushed, as we file into the lab and take seats in a row of metal folding chairs. Instead, we spend the next hour and a half listening to the teacher drone on about something called polyploidy and hybridization. Major snooze fest.

When class is finally over, we get a tour of the gardens, but they have to rush us through it because the buses are waiting to take us back to the middle school. Everyone we pass seems to know who May is, which shouldn't surprise me, I guess, because she's been coming here all spring. Not to mention her older brother is some kind of big shot senior here. If only Layla were an Earth, she could have paved the way for me a little bit. Whatever. At least I have May. Every time someone stops to say "hi" to her, she introduces me as her "best friend CJ," and they immediately welcome me and say how much I'm going to love it at DES.

If only I knew for sure I was going to be here.

5

Devon has a Sparkplugs meeting after school, so I take the long way home, stopping at a convenience store to pick up some magazines. I have twenty-three dollars in my pocket—basically all the money I have in the world—and I'm prepared to spend it. I figure that if I'm serious about finding out my source, I'm going to have to invest in some major research materials.

I browse the racks and pick out the required reading for an unidentified girl my age: Teen Earth, TeenBreeze, and Aquateen. There are no girl Fire mags, which makes sense, if you consider that there are, like, no girl Fires. Not much of a market for that. The total comes to $14.76. Ouch.

I bury the magazines in my backpack and head for home. Our house sits at the top of a hill on a quiet, tree-lined street. It's a cavernous, four-bedroom Victorian with a wraparound porch, steep-pitched gabled roof, and gingerbread woodwork under the eaves. Real storybook material.

I guess I should say five-bedroom, if you count Layla's room on the third floor, which is really just the walk-up attic. She used to have the bedroom next to mine on the second floor, but when Airhead and the boys moved in, someone had to move. The boys couldn't share a room because it was too dangerous for Matty with Devon fireballing in his sleep, and neither of the boys was old enough to be all alone on the third floor. That left two choices: Layla and I could share a room on the second floor, or one of us could move up to the attic. Neither of us wanted to share, and since Layla is older, she got first pick.

I was shocked at first when Layla picked the attic, with that steep set of stairs and no bathroom. But now I see the genius of her ways. It's private up there … and quiet. It's probably the only quiet place in the whole house.

When I get home, Airhead is in the backyard with some construction guys, pointing at trees, measuring things, and planting little orange flags around the yard. My mom is watering her flower garden with Matty following after her, spritzing the flowers with his fingertips.

Show off.

My mom waves when she sees me and comes inside. I go upstairs to my room, and she follows me in.

"Hi, sweetie. How was the last day of school?"

"Did you know May was going to Gray Rock this summer?"

"No. I knew it was a possibility, but—"

"Great. Now I'll be all alone at Medley."

19

"Celeste. Sit down. We need to talk about camp." I sit down on the bed.

"What about it?"

"I think maybe we should consider some other options for this summer. If you go to Medley, you're going to be the oldest one there. I think it might be a little boring for you."

"You're acting like I have a choice. I can't even apply to any of the source camps, so what's your point?"

"Well, Rainie Langford goes to Fluidity, and her mom says they have a great summer program for kids your age."

The Langfords live across the street from us. They named their kids Harmony and Rainbow, which should give you some idea what they're like. The parents are like, fifty, and they still won't identify. Won't … or can't. I've heard about people whose source never comes out, but usually that's considered a bad thing. Like a time-to-see-a-doctor bad thing. But the Langfords don't seem to care. They say they don't believe everyone has to identify. Whatever.

Rainie, their daughter, is my age, and she's unidentified, too. Only, she's like, proud of it. We used to play together when I first moved here. Now I hardly ever see her because she goes to private school at Fluidity. But each year she gets weirder and weirder. Lately, she wears these ridiculous flowered sundresses all the time—right out of the 1950s—with big black leather boots that go up to her knees, and leather gloves, even in the summer. Her older brother, Harm, is not much better. At least he's identified. He's a Fire, like Devon. I see him across the street in the garage, making some sort of weird art with recycled newspaper that he rips into different shapes and burns around the edges.

This is who my mom wants me hanging out with?

"Mom, you know how I feel about that place."

"I know you're not that thrilled about the idea, but I think if you give it a chance, it could be really good for you. Who knows, you might end up liking it enough to stay."

"Stay? Where? Freakidity? You've got to be kidding me. Was this her idea?"

"This has nothing to do with Jackie. This is about what's best for you. This is a wonderful opportunity for you to get to know yourself in an open, accepting environment."

"Okay, now you sound just like her. You would never make me do this if she weren't here."

"That's not true. Don't make this about Jackie. You could really benefit from this. Not everyone has the luxury—"

"You know what? Forget it. I'll go. You're never going to listen to me anyway."

"I know you're skeptical now, but promise me you'll give it a chance."

"I said I would go, okay?"

"Okay. That's all I ask. I think you're going to get something out of this. I really do."

Don't bet on it.

She kisses me on the cheek and walks out of the room. Rover bends around to see her go.

"Traitor," I say to the plant.

6

I text May immediately. "CALL ME!" She dials me back before I even put the phone down.

"Is everything okay?" she asks.

"Only if you consider me going to Fluidity Camp with Rainie Langford okay," I say.

"Freakidity? No way!"

"No joke. Just when I thought it couldn't get any worse."

"Don't worry, I have some tie-dyed shirts you can borrow. No, wait, how about a flowered sundress and some boots?"

Before I know it, I'm smiling. That's my May.

"Okay, stop. This is NOT funny. How come you get to go to the best Earth camp in the state, and I'm stuck 'finding myself' at the local freak farm?"

"CJ, can I ask you something?"

"Yeah, sure. What is it?"

"What if I made it up?"

"Made what up?"

"My source." She's whispering now.

"May, what are you talking about?"

"I mean, it's hard to know when you're an Earth, you know. There's no gills, no floating up into the air while you sleep. I just thought, I'll say I know, you know, and then my parents will stop bugging me about it. It's bound to happen soon anyway. But at camp, with all those Earth counselors watching me, what if I can't do it?"

"But May, you have to be an Earth, your whole family—"

"They don't look at me, CJ. They don't."

"Who?"

"The plants. It's like I'm invisible in my own house. My parents, my brother … the plants all bend to them. Not me."

"That doesn't mean anything. They're older than you. They have a stronger pull. It's impossible to tell when you're in the room with them. You said yourself that when you're alone, they bend to you."

"I mean, this fall, I thought so. The minute I mentioned it to my mom, that was it. She was on the phone to the school, signing me up for Earth classes, filling out applications to Gray Rock. But now I'm not so sure."

"You're just nervous because this is your first time going away to camp. You'll be fine. There's no way you're not an Earth. No way."

"I hope you're right."

"I know I'm right. You're gonna ROCK it. Get it? … rock … Gray Rock?"

"Okay, that's the worst joke I've ever heard. But, thank you. I'm going to miss you this summer."

"Me too."

"Hey, can you come over to dinner tomorrow?"

"I think so."

"Good. I'd hate to spend my last night here without you."

We hang up.

I can't believe that I'm not going to see her for eight weeks. Then I think about what she said. No gills, no levitating. If you have to fake it, Earth is definitely the way to go. Why sit around and wait for your source to come to you? If you want something, go out and get it.

I take out my copy of Teen Earth and start to flip through it. On the "What's HOT Now" list: braided belts, Earth-friendly nail polish remover, nude lipsticks.

Hunh.

I doubt that wearing nude lipstick is going to help me get into source school, but hey, you never know. Next, I scan the table of contents for helpful articles. Among the selections: "How to Flirt with an Earth," "Why Earth Boys are Easy: 10 Easy Steps to Make Him Fall for You," "The Plants All Bend to Look at Me, Why Doesn't He?" Okaaay.

This would all be very helpful if I wanted an Earth for a boyfriend, but not so much when it comes to learning how to be one myself. I'm starting to think that I need to rethink my approach ... and that I just wasted fourteen dollars and seventy-six cents.

7

The next morning at breakfast, Airhead is all in a tizzy.

"Six inches!" she shouts. Instinctively, we all grab our juice cups as she sends a gust of warm air across the table. "Six inches over the rear setback, and we have to go to the council for a variance!"

"Jackie," says my mom, "this is just a little bump in the road. Nothing to get upset about."

"Really? Have you forgotten who's in the open seat this term?"

"Myrna is a reasonable person. I'm sure—"

"Myrna Braddock is as far from reasonable as you can get. She is going to drag her feet all the way. I've got to call Gwen. She'll be the swing vote on this one." With that, Airhead breezes out of the room. We all exhale and take our hands off our cups.

"What is a swing boat?" asks Devon.

"A swing vote, Devon, is someone who … who breaks a tie if the rest of the town council is split evenly." That's all Devon needs to hear to know that he could not care less about swing votes.

"Can I be 'scused?" he asks.

"Sure." says my mom. "Please bring your plate to the sink."

"Me too?" says Matty.

"Of course, sweetie. Careful with that plate."

"Why would the council care if we want a pool?" Layla asks.

"Well," says my mom, "they are in charge of making sure we develop our property in a responsible way, according to town law."

"It's not against the law to have a pool." I say. "Plenty of people in Darwin have pools."

"No, you're right. But there are rules about where you can put them on your property. Ours is going to be a little too close to the property line, so we have to get a special permit."

"What does she have against Myrna Braddock?" asks Layla. "I thought Myrna was a friend of yours."

"Myrna is my friend, but she has very strong views about what's right for this town and for the environment, and not everybody agrees with them."

"If people don't like her, how did she get elected?" I ask.

"She wasn't elected, exactly. She was appointed to the open seat. Don't they teach you this stuff in school?"

"Yeah, yeah, I know. The Earth Party gets to appoint the fifth council member," I say.

"No, not the Earth Party, the party with the most identified members appoints the open seat."

"Well, that's the Earth Party, right?"

"Well, yes, it happens to be—"

"Has it ever *not* happened to be?"

"Not in Darwin, but—"

"Okay, so the Earth Party gets the open seat."

"Fine. As it happens, in Darwin, the Earth Party has the open seat. That doesn't mean they get to do whatever they want. Each of the four major parties is guaranteed one seat on the council. That means the party with the open seat needs the agreement of at least one council member from another party to have a majority."

"The swing vote?" I ask.

"Exactly," she says. Then she gets a twinkle in her eye. Bad news, people. "What a great opportunity this will be for the two of you to see your town government in action."

"The two of who? See what in action?" I ask.

"You and Layla should go to the meeting with me and Jackie. It'll be better than any classroom."

Layla makes a sign that means she is either going to slit her throat, or mine. Not sure I want to find out which. Time to change the subject.

"Um, mom? May asked if I could go over to her house for dinner tonight. Is that okay?"

"Of course. How nice. I know you're going to miss her this summer." She pats my head as if to say, you poor, poor thing. This, of course, annoys me. I know I'm about to have the lamest summer ever, but could she just not rub it in?

8

I know to wear something nice when I go to May's for dinner. Let's just say, there's no way we will be eating hot dogs off plastic plates.

Sure enough, when I walk through the front door, I know I'm in for a treat. May's house is set up like a mini-DES. The rooms of the house surround a large, glassed-in center courtyard. But instead of having a greenhouse roof, this one is open to the sky.

Tonight the sliding glass doors to the courtyard are wide open, and May's mom has set up a table outside. China, silverware, crystal goblets, the works. The table sits under a grape arbor. Strings of tiny white lights adorn the vines, making the glass and silver sparkle. Ivy—or is it more grape vines?—encircles the table legs and snakes its way up the backs of the chairs.

"Oh, honey, don't you look nice," May's mom chirps as I walk out into the courtyard.

"Hi, Mrs. Jacobs ... Mr. Jacobs," I nod at May's parents.

"Why don't we all sit down," suggests May's mother, and she claps her hands together like some kind of audio-exclamation point. She gestures toward the table where bowls of chilled cucumber soup sit ready at each place setting.

May's parents take their seats at the ends of the table. I grab a spot next to May. May's brother, Aaron, and his girlfriend, Jenna, round out the other side. I watch as the ivy curls around to caress the shoulders of the table guests. My ivy doesn't even know I'm alive. I turn to check out May, who is fidgeting uncomfortably in her chair, no doubt to distract from the lack of ivy activity behind her. I catch her eye, and she turns bright pink. I wink at her, and she breaks into a smile.

I'm about to sample the soup when May's mother sets her sights on me and goes straight for the jugular.

"So, Celeste, where will you be at camp this summer?" she asks.

May jumps in, "Mom! She doesn't, she's not—"

"I'm not identified yet," I say. "I guess I'm going to, um, Fluidity."

"Oh. I'm sorry, dear. I didn't know. Well, that is … that is—"

"What my wife is trying to say is that we hear wonderful things about Fluidity," says Mr. Jacobs. "Don't we, Rachel?"

"Of course we do. I'm sure you will have a wonderful summer. And, of course, we are ecstatic that May will be joining Aaron—and Jenna—at Gray Rock this summer. You did keep us in suspense for a while, though, didn't you, darling?"

May turns pink all over again.

"Ignore her," says Aaron, as he grabs a handful of grapes from the lattice behind him and pops them into his mouth. "You are gonna love GR."

"Oh, yeah," Jenna adds, "GR is the best! You spend all day outside, planting, swimming, hiking. And then there's the big harvest fair at the end with all the parents and stuff."

"The harvest fair is pretty great," May says in my direction. "I've gone to that every year since Aaron started going there. Maybe you can come up for it." Her eyes turn in her mother's direction.

"We'll see. Okay, dear? The fair is still a long way off."

I'll take that as a no.

May's mom continues, "May, sweetie, why don't you help me clear the soup, and we'll move on to the next course."

Four courses later, I'm barely able to roll myself to the curb, where my mom is waiting with the engine running. When I step outside, I'm immediately cold, even though we have been in an open courtyard the whole night. I miss the cozy glow of the twinkly lights and warmth of the grape arbor.

Imagine, getting to eat dinner in an oasis every night. Oh, and no one shoots fireballs across the table.

May is so lucky.

She walks me to the curb, stopping to grab my hand before I get into the car.

"I'm not sure if I'm going to have cell service at GR, but text me anyway, okay?" she says.

"You bet. Wish me luck with the hippies."

"Good luck!"

We hug. I hop in the back seat and wave good-bye as my mom pulls away.

It feels so final.

I take a deep breath. I survived eleven years of life before I met May Jacobs. I can survive one summer without her, right?

Besides, how bad can it be?

9

I almost walk out when I see the goats.

My mom and I are on a tour of the Fluidity campus. The school is located on a farm on the edge of Darwin. I've driven by the entrance a million times. It has a gate of hand-carved wood, with the word "Fluidity" burned into it in a flowing script. This is my first time inside.

When we passed through the gate this morning, it was like entering another world. The road turned to dirt, winding its way through the trees so that it was impossible to see what was ahead. The sun flickered in and out of view through the leaves, making an ever-changing pattern on the hood of my mom's SUV. Suddenly, we emerged from the trees to a view of a pond, surrounded by a group of old farmhouses and a giant barn. A dirt path encircled the pond and connected each of the buildings. Behind the barn, I could see the orderly rows of a garden stretching into the distance.

Now, a middle-aged woman with short, graying hair in a turquoise jumpsuit is leading us around the path, pointing out each of the buildings. Meeting house, dining hall, library, communal garden, goat barn … GOAT BARN?

"Here is where we tend our goats, Raja, Pippa, Orzo, and Melanie. They are great friends to us, and they supply milk for the school." The tour guide smiles at us, as if she hasn't just said something totally insane. The goats are preoccupied with eating everything in sight. Orzo looks up at us and starts to pee. Melanie bleats.

I make a mental note not to drink the milk in the cafeteria.

I shoot my mom a look, and she widens her eyes and tilts her head at me, as if to say, "Be polite, and just give it a chance." At least that's what I think she would say if the Fluidity lady weren't standing right there.

"Here at Fluidity, we exist in a completely cooperative, communal way. We each make a daily contribution, according to the Contribution Chart."

Chores. Great. Just what I want to do on my summer vacation. I might as well be at home. At least there the chores don't include scooping up goat poop.

"And the remaining time is spent doing personal exploration, relationship building, and mind/body synchronization."

My mom smiles, apparently fascinated by this whole incomprehensible mess.

"Okay. Any questions?" the tour guide asks. Yeah, where's the nearest exit?

"No, thank you," my mom says. "It all sounds so wonderful. I guess, just one thing. What is it that you do for mind/body synchronization, exactly?" Good question.

"That can include any number of activities that blend mental focus and physical exertion ... yoga, dance, tai chi ... and we are always open to a camper developing his or her own mind/body experience. We have one young man who has become quite adept at unicycle juggling. Now he can go down stairs without even dropping a beanbag."

Seriously? All this place needs is a big top tent and a cotton candy machine, and we can start charging for admission. I wonder if the goats know any tricks.

"Well, Celeste," says the tour guide, looking like she might spontaneously hug me, "we at Fluidity are over the moon that you will be joining us this summer. Just don't forget to bring a bathing suit, your imagination, and your own reusable water bottle. We try to stay away from disposable products."

Over the moon? You got that right.

"SAVE ME! There are goats!" I text to May during the car ride home. No response. Cell phone service must be pretty weak, or nonexistent, wherever May is because this is my fifth text since she's been gone, and I've had no response. I'm guessing that whatever she's doing at Gray Rock, it doesn't involve a unicycle and beanbags.

10

It's the night before my first day of camp, and the rest of my family is downstairs eating dinner. I excused myself early to go lie down in my room, but instead, I'm sitting at the computer in my mom and Airhead's room, hoping no one will notice.

From downstairs, I hear Airhead yell, "Devon, stop it! Matty, sit down. Eat your chicken nuggets, or no dessert tonight!" A cabinet door blows shut, and Matty starts to cry. Yeah, I'm pretty sure no one will notice.

I turn on the computer and log in with my mom's password. Serenity. Mom, so predictable, yet so adorable. I hop onto Google, type "How to fake being an Earth," and press search. No use beating around the bush, right?

Over two million results. Wow, guess I'm not the first person to try this. It could take years to sort through all these. Oh well, what choice do I have?

WikiHow has a few articles on "how to train your plants to bend to you" or "gardening for the aspiring Earth." I click on the first article and start to read: "The key to creating a bond between you and your plants is to spend time with them. Read to them (poetry by Robert Frost is a favorite). Sing a song. Immerse yourself in their world. Go barefoot in your garden. Rub your hands and feet in the soil." All this is pretty basic stuff, but at least it's a place to start.

YouTube has videos of Earths coaxing their house plants to contort themselves while "Limbo Rock" or "Macarena" plays in the background. Hysterical, but not very helpful. For fun, I click on a couple of videos showing Airs levitating during sleep in unfortunate situations. One girl falls asleep on a lawn chair by a pool and wakes up screaming when she plunges into the water. Another guy falls asleep in a meeting, and instead of waking him up, his co-workers film him on their cell phones as he floats right into the middle of the conference table. He wakes up totally mortified with his head on a tray of bagels. Hilarious!

I look across the room at my mom and Airhead's bed. It's a big four-poster, but instead of a canopy, there's mosquito netting stretched across the top of the posts and around all four sides, with zippers so you can climb in and out like a tent. This is Airhead's invention. Apparently, when Airs go into REM sleep, they have a tendency to levitate off the bed. Most normal people buy a weighted blanket and call it a day. But Airhead doesn't like them. Says they are "oppressive" or something. So she invented this tent where she can float freely without drifting away from the bed and crashing to the floor. Why does she have to be so weird?

11

It's another restless night. I dream that I'm walking toward the bus stop at the end of my street. Kids are approaching from every direction. Their footsteps are oddly in unison. As they reach the intersection, they break off into groups. I look for May, Layla, anyone I know, but none of the faces are clear to me. I don't recognize anyone.

The buses start to arrive. Four of them pull up. They sit idling at the curb. I look for the DES bus, but none of the buses are marked. The kids start piling on. "Where's the DES bus?" I ask. No one answers me. They're in a hurry, I guess. STOP walking and ANSWER me! I try to push to the front, so that I can ask the driver, but the crowd is too thick. I'm being trampled, suffocated.

I wake up sweaty and annoyed. What time is it? Am I late for school? Then it sets in. It's summer. And I'm going to Fluidity Camp. Ugh.

I get dressed in my bohemian best … a tee shirt with a rainbow-colored peace sign on the front and a pair of shorts. Hey, when in Rome.

Downstairs, Airhead and the boys are at the table eating breakfast. Airhead says, "Morning, CJ." I hate when she calls me that. Only May calls me that. I grunt something like "good morning" and stick my head in the fridge, looking for OJ.

"Sorry, CJ, we just drank the last of the juice. There's some frozen mix if you want to whip some up."

Grunt.

"Your mom went to drop Layla off. She'll be back in a minute to get you. Your backpack is by the door."

"Okay," I manage.

I grab a granola bar from the pantry and head for the front door. My cell phone rings.

"Hi, mom."

"Hi, sweetie. How is your morning going? Did you eat breakfast?"

"Yeah, I ate something," I lie.

"Celeste, I completely forgot that Layla's swim trials are today. I thought they were next week. So I need to stay. But I called the Langfords, and they can give you a ride to camp. Just run across the street and ring the bell. They're expecting you."

"What? You always do this—"

"Celeste, I know you're upset. But I promised Layla I would be at her swim trials. I will be there to drive you tomorrow. Plus, you'll be with Rainie. She can show you where to go. She's been going there for years."

The tears are coming now, and there's nothing I can do to stop them. "Why can't I just wait for you? I can be late. Who cares if I'm there on time anyway?"

"Celeste, you should be there for the morning meeting. You don't want to miss a chance to meet all the counselors and the other kids."

"I don't care if I meet them! I didn't even want to go in the first place!"

"Sweetie, the trials take hours. If you're not comfortable going with the Langfords, Jackie can take you after she drops the boys." Could it be any more obvious that I'm last on everybody's list?

"Never mind. I'm NOT going with Airhead Jackie—"

"Celeste!"

"Sorry, sorry! Never mind. I'll go across the street."

"Okay, honey. Be nice! I'll be there this afternoon to pick you up, I promise. I can't wait to hear all about it."

"Okay, bye."

I hang up and face my fate. Carpooling with the Langfords. Do they even have a car, or will we be pedaling our way to camp on solar-power-assisted mopeds?

Airhead walks over to me, "CJ, is everything okay?"

"I'm fine," I say, although clearly I have been crying. "And my name's Celeste."

"I'm sorry, Celeste. I guess I'm so used to May calling you that—"

"Well, you're not May," I say, and I walk out the door.

12

I knock on the Langfords' front door and then stand there—like an idiot—for what feels like an hour, fiddling with my backpack and tucking my hair behind my ears, until Rainie finally answers the door. Rainie's hair is short and black, and she has these long bangs that sweep across her face and almost cover her emerald green eyes. She would be pretty if you could actually see her face.

I realize that I'm staring at her, and I haven't even said hello. But, how do you say hello to someone you have basically been ignoring for two years?

"Hey," I say.

"Hey."

Rainie is wearing jean cutoffs and a gray tank top. Same boots. Same gloves. She looks like she's off to some kind of weird military camp.

"What, no sundress?" I say. Oops. I don't think I meant for that to be out loud.

"What did you say?"

"Sorry. I just meant, when I see you around, you're usually wearing a dress."

"You notice a lot for someone that hasn't said 'hi' to me in years."

"You're the one who went off to private school, not me."

I can see the heat rising in her face. Then, suddenly, she puts her palms up like she is meditating, closes her eyes, and lets out a deep breath. She opens her eyes again. "Let's just stay out of each other's way, okay?"

"Sounds good to me," I say.

She looks back inside the house, "Dad, Harm, hurry up! We're gonna be late for morning meeting!"

I sit in the back seat of the car, behind Rainie's dad. Harm is in the front passenger seat, with Rainie directly behind him. No one's talking. The only thing that breaks the silence is the muffled sound of rap music that occasionally seeps out from Harm's headphones. I steal a look at Rainie. She's looking steadily out the window. Her dad starts to hum something that I can only identify as vaguely country, apparently unaware that this is the most uncomfortable car ride ever.

It wasn't always this way.

I first moved here two years ago, the summer after my parents got divorced. At that time, my mom alternated between spending the day on the couch, crying, and darting around the house like a maniac, cleaning and unpacking boxes. On the couch days, Rainie's mom would come over, cook meals, and comfort my mom, leaving Harm, Rainie, Layla, and me to our own devices.

Harm and Layla were too old to be bothered with me or Rainie, or even each other for that matter. Harm mostly hung out in the family room, playing video games and doing his art projects, while Layla stayed in her bedroom, reading, or writing in her journal. That left Rainie and me to play together.

And so we did. We listened to my mom's old records over and over again. Diana Ross, Fleetwood Mac, the Beatles, Blondie. We performed concerts for our moms in the living room. She was always Diana Ross, and I was Blondie ... because she has dark hair, and I have blonde hair, obviously.

We constructed elaborate worlds together. Sometimes, we were pioneers, living in a cabin in the woods, hunting and gathering, and making mud pies to sustain ourselves. The pine trees behind the house generated a thick carpet of dried-up, orange pine needles that could be gathered into huge piles and shaped into the walls of a fort.

We drew chalk masterpieces on the driveway, only to wash them away with the hose, having decided that we were actually professional car washers, scrubbing and buffing my mom's SUV until it shined.

In the basement, it was roller derby. We raced around the poles as Diana crooned the words to "Upside Down."

We made friendship bracelets. We sold lemonade by the curb. We laughed.

Rainie basically turned what could've been the worst summer of my life into ... the best.

Then school started. I went to the local public school. Rainie went to Fluidity. At first, we played together after school and on weekends. But soon, I had soccer games, band, dance class. I was making new friends, too. School friends. May.

With everything I had going on, I didn't have hours to spend lying around listening to records anymore. Not to mention, my school friends didn't exactly have the best impression of Fluidity. Word around school was that Fluidity kids were weird, hippie kids, whose parents looked down on the public schools, and down on us. Pretty soon, I started to agree with them. I mean, look at what happened to Rainie ... the weird outfits, the strange breathing. After a while, Rainie and I barely acknowledged each other. And I barely noticed.

I look up as the car pulls into the driveway at Fluidity. A big cardboard sign with rainbow-colored letters welcomes us to camp and points us in the direction of the meeting house. Here goes nothing.

13

The meeting house is a long, single-story building with one huge room inside, like a gymnasium. Only instead of a basketball court, the floor is painted with some funky symbol in the middle.

"What's that?" I ask Rainie. In spite of our pact to stay away from each other, I'm curious, and I don't have anyone else to ask.

"It's an 'om,'" she says. It sounds like "Rome" without the "R."

"A what?"

"It's Tibetan. There's a little bit of chanting at morning meeting. You'll get used to it."

Rainie and Harm sit down cross-legged in the mass of campers and counselors that are assembled in a rough circle around the om. I fall back behind them by a few rows and do the same. The lady from the tour stands up in the middle of the circle.

"Welcome, everyone. I'm Liz, the camp director. I see many familiar faces this summer, and a couple of new faces as well. Would Celeste and Tyrone please stand up?" Oh, no, please, no. I hate when people look at me.

As soon as I see Tyrone, I know I needn't have worried. Not a single person in this room is going to be looking at me. Tyrone is striking. He is probably close to six feet tall, muscular, with dark brown skin, brown eyes, and a face out of a magazine. The hair on his head is shaved close to the scalp, and his neck and arms are littered with small scars and burn marks. Some of these have been tattooed into black starbursts or comets or something, barely visible on his dark skin. On his left index finger, I see a tattoo of a lit match. The black ink flames curl up his hand and around his wrist and forearm. He looks too old to be here. I guess he could be Harm's age. But how did he end up at Fluidity? He doesn't really strike me as the meditation type.

Tyrone and I stand, and the group says in unison, "Hi, Celeste. Hi, Tyrone." We sit down.

Whew. That wasn't so bad.

Liz continues, "We gather here each morning to share the important news of the day, and to feel the strength of our community before we set off on our individual journeys. Today's announcements: weather permitting, yoga will be held in the pavilion at eleven, guided by Shanti." A woman next to Liz stands up and waves. "And Ben will be storytelling in the afternoon at the picnic tables." A wave from Ben. "Watercolor easels and sketch pads will be by the pond, as usual. I will be down at the dock all morning, administering the swim test for those of you who want your swim bracelet. The meeting house will be open as a meditation space. No cell phone use in here, please. Would anyone like to share anything this morning?"

I can only assume no one volunteers. I can't say for sure because I'm staring intently at my feet, hoping I'm not about to be called on again.

"Alright, everyone. Let's chant. We repeat the sacred syllables, Om Ah Hung."

Everyone around me is grabbing each other's hands. The girl in front of me reaches back and grabs one of mine. I look around but there is no one else near me, so I leave the other one in my lap.

OOOOOOoooooooooommmmm. The sound fills the room. It seeps into my fingertips, my knees, my eyes, my skin, until it reaches my bones. My whole body vibrates from the hum of everyone's voice coming together in a low rumble.

AAAAAAaaaaaaaaahhhhhh. This sound is higher. It makes me feel strangely transparent. The sound is a beam of light, shining through me. I imagine that it lifts me off the ground, like the parachute that we used to use in gym class, waving and flapping the edges until it filled with air.

HHhuuuuuuuunnnnnnnggg. It lowers me back down again. A soft, slow landing. A flower petal, weaving left, then right, until it lands silently on a bed of grass.

I open my eyes and look around me, slowly reorienting to my surroundings. "Welcome to Fluidity Camp," says Liz.

Whoa.

14

I catch up to Rainie as everyone files out of the meeting house. "What now?" I ask.

"What do you mean, what now?"

"I mean, what am I supposed to do next?"

"Whatever you want."

"Whatever I want?"

"Yeah. Like, figure out what you want to do, and do it."

I stare at her blankly. At Medley, every minute was scheduled: arts and crafts from 9:00-10:00; morning snack, 10:00-10:30; soccer, 10:30-11:30 ... you get the idea.

"You'll figure it out," she says, and she walks away.

Not quite sure what to do, I follow a large stream of people heading towards the building that holds the kitchen and dining hall. Inside the front door, a group of kids is gathered around a big poster on the wall. The Contribution Chart. I look for my name on the list. Under Monday, it says, "weed the garden."

Weed the garden. I can do that. In fact, my mom's been *making* me do that since I was six years old. No sweat.

When I get to the garden, it's the size of an Olympic swimming pool. The beds are arranged in long rows, separated by aisles about three feet wide. Smaller paths intersect the aisles and create breaks in the vegetable beds. I glance around at the signs marking the beds: peas, squash, tomatoes, carrots, beets ... the list goes on and on. I hope I'm not supposed to weed this whole thing by myself.

Oh, well. According to the article on WikiHow, I'm supposed to be spending my time communing with the plants, so here goes. I take off my shoes and dig my toes into the earth. It's cool and still slightly damp from the morning dew. I sniff the air, wondering if I'm going to be stepping in fertilizer, or worse. I don't smell anything other than the slightly moldy scent of wet earth, so I grab a small wheelbarrow and start down the first row, pulling up weeds and tossing them into my cart.

No sweat? I should have said, lots of sweat. Because after weeding one row of green beans, I'm drenched. When I look up, I see Tyrone a couple of rows over, trying his hand at weeding. The only problem is he's pulling up more beets and carrots than weeds. It's a massacre.

"Um, you're not really supposed to pull those ones," I say.

"Huh?"

"The vegetables. You're not supposed to pick them yet. You're gonna kill them. We're just supposed to, you know, pull up the weeds and leave the other stuff."

He laughs. "I'd be happy to. 'Cept they all look the same to me."

"You've never weeded before?"

This time just a smirk. "Yeah. We do mad weeding in the Meadow."

The Meadow is a neighborhood in New Preston where it seems, ironically, that not even grass will grow. I've seen it on TV before, with its tall, rectangular apartment buildings and cement playgrounds. I've never been there though. My dad says it's off limits because it's too dangerous.

"Here, let me show you," I offer.

"Thanks," he says, then he looks down at my bare feet, which are caked with dirt. "Am I supposed to take my shoes off, too?" he asks.

"Um, no, that's okay. I just, um, had blisters, so … you can keep your shoes on."

I identify a few plants for him and we start down the rows. We don't talk much. When he comes across a plant he doesn't know, he just points at it, and I do a thumbs up if he is supposed to pull it. Before we know it, we've done the whole garden.

"Well, Tyrone, it was a pleasure working with you," I say, holding out my hand. He shakes it.

"It's Matchstick."

"What?"

"Only my grandma calls me Tyrone. I'm Match." He holds out the finger with the matchstick tattoo and a small blue flame appears at the tip of his finger.

I look confused.

"Yeah, so you're wondering why a Fire has burn marks all over him? It's because I'm not a Fire, really. I've only got this one finger that works. Been that way since I was twelve. I keep testing it though." He gestures towards the burn marks on his arms. "So, they started calling me Matchstick."

It's the most he's said to me all morning. I should say something now, something insightful, yet witty, something that lets him know that I feel like an outsider here, too.

"Oh, cool," I say. Argh.

He laughs again. "A'ight. Catch you later, Celeste." With that, he wanders off toward the barn.

After I recover from my utter humiliation in front of Match, I decide that I need to do something about the thick layer of dirt that has built up on my feet and hands. I change into my swimming attire—a one-piece suit and a pair of swim shorts—and head for the pond.

Liz is stationed near the end of the dock, administering the swim test. This is one test I have no fear of failing. I have gone swimming nearly every day of the summer for as long as I can remember. When it's my turn with Liz, I dive in, enjoying the adrenaline rush as the cold water envelops my body. I descend to the bottom of the pond, then push off the ground to propel myself to the surface. I immediately regret that decision, as my foot sinks into a thick layer of muck. I'm starting to doubt whether I will emerge from this swim much cleaner than when I came in. I might as well complete the test, anyway. I follow Liz's instructions … crawl, back float, tread water … until she declares me fit for a red rubber bracelet—my ticket to free swim for the rest of the summer.

I swim to the square wooden raft in the center of the pond and climb on to survey my surroundings. Sunbathers lounge on towels in the sandy area by the dock. Further to the right, on the lawn, someone has organized a game of ultimate Frisbee. Others sit and read, or sketch, in the shade of the trees that line the pond.

To the left of the swim dock, a large, rectangular deck with a roof extends out over the water. The pavilion.

I see Shanti setting up her mat. One by one, campers begin to join her. I swim to shore and walk the short distance to the pavilion. I grab a mat from a bin by the entrance and unroll it in an available spot near the back.

Shanti starts us off with some breathing exercises, which immediately reminds me of Rainie's little breathing episode this morning. What is it with the breathing? Okay, I can understand that it is healthy to breathe in and out, but what is with the noise everyone is making? The pavilion sounds like a giant steam kettle about to blow.

Shanti starts to take us through the yoga poses. I've done this once or twice before with my mom and Layla, so it's not completely foreign to me, but I still find myself craning my neck around a lot, trying to see what I'm supposed to be doing. Each time, Shanti comes over to me and gently realigns my neck.

"Don't worry so much about what others are doing," she says. "Your yoga practice is about you and no one else. Do what feels right to you."

"But I don't even know what some of these poses are," I say.

"I'll help you with that," she says. "The most important thing is that you listen to your body and don't do anything to hurt yourself." She smiles. "I'm pretty sure your neck is not made to turn 180 degrees."

"Okay," I say. "As long as you don't mind if I'm doing it wrong."

"If you listen to your body, there's no such thing as doing it wrong," she says. "It's when you overthink it that you get into trouble."

I close my eyes and try not to look at anyone else. I bend and twist, following Shanti's commands to the best of my ability. Her tone is so soothing that makes me want to curl up and go to sleep. In fact, I nearly do fall asleep at the end, while we are all lying on our backs in relaxation pose. I have to admit, between the swimming and the yoga, I'm feeling good. Better than I have in a long time, in fact.

After another dip in the pond to rinse off the yoga sweat, I head to the library. Nobody is at the desk, so I grab a book of Robert Frost poems and head back to the pond. Now, for the right audience … I remember passing a willow tree down by the water, and it seems like the perfect place for what I have to do.

Back down by the pond, I duck inside the willow, caressing its dangling branches with my hands as I pass through them. I position myself at the base of the tree, sitting on the ground and leaning with my back against the trunk. I take off my shoes and rub my feet into the ground. "Ready, Willow?" I say. "I hope you like Robert Frost." I start to read:

The Tuft of Flowers

I went to turn the grass once after one
Who mowed it in the dew before the sun.
The dew was gone that made his blade so keen
Before I came to view the leveled scene.

I looked for him behind an isle of trees;
I listened for his whetstone on the breeze.

But he had gone his way, the grass all mown,
And I must be, as he had been, —alone,

'As all must be,' I said within my heart,
'Whether they work together or apart.'

But as I said it, swift there passed me by
On noiseless wing a 'wildered butterfly,

Seeking with memories grown dim o'er night
Some resting flower of yesterday's delight ...

I look up, and Rainie is standing at the edge of the willow, staring at me.

"Do you always read out loud to yourself?" she asks.

"Only when I feel like it." I answer. Real smooth, Celeste.

"Well, do you mind doing it somewhere else? This is kind of my spot."

"Oh, sorry. I didn't know."

Suddenly, a cow bell rings, and Rainie turns to look behind her. Everyone around us is making a bee-line for the kitchen. "It's no big deal," she says. "I'm just in the middle of a sketch, so I need to sit here after lunch, okay?"

"Okay," I say.

"Thanks," she says.

She turns around and joins the crowd heading up the hill. I follow a short distance behind. Inside, the kitchen looks like I imagine almost any farmhouse kitchen would look. Fridge, stove, industrial-sized double sink. A large, wooden butcher block serves as an island in the middle of the room. The only difference is that one wall has been opened up and replaced with a countertop that is open to the hallway. The hallway side of the counter is fitted with a metal shelf for sliding food trays. I join the line that has begun to stretch down the hall towards the door.

When I finally reach the counter, I grab a tray and load it up with the only thing that looks somewhat recognizable to me: salad and something the cook calls "momo" dumplings. I fill a glass with water, avoiding the milk jug as planned, and head to the dining room. The room is filled with long wooden tables, surrounded by benches and mismatched chairs. I spot Match eating alone at the end of a table in the corner and decide to join him. He's the closest thing I have to a friend here at this point.

He looks up as I approach and nods, presumably signaling that I'm free to pull up a chair. We eat next to each other in silence. It turns out that eating with Match is just about the same as eating alone.

My eyes wander, and I see Rainie across the room. She is sitting next to Harm at a table of full-time Fluidity kids, mostly girls, who are practically pawing each other out of the way to get Harm's attention. Rainie looks bored. She looks up and her eyes meet mine. I turn away quickly, pretending to enjoy my dumplings more than any other food I have ever tasted. I will not give her the satisfaction of knowing that I'm about to cry I'm so lonely. No offense, Match.

Match speaks. "You like that guy or something?"

"What guy?"

"The guy you were staring at over there."

"Harm? No, I wasn't looking at him. I was just looking around. You know, you two might get along. He's a Fire."

"He is? What's he doing here then? I thought this place was for unidentifieds."

"Oh, his parents think everyone should go to Fluidity. They probably think it's a bad thing that he's identified. Pretty much just take everything you know about the world, and his parents think the opposite."

"Hunh."

"Come on, I'll introduce you."

All eyes are on us, or I should say, on Match, as we cross the room. I walk over and plant myself right between Harm and Rainie, turning my back to her.

"Harm, this is Match. I told him you might show him a Fire trick or two."

"Hey, man, seriously?" says Harm, his eyes lighting up. "You leaning towards Fire? We don't get many around here, with all the peace and love stuff going on."

Soon, Match and Harm are off in their own little world, and I'm left standing there, like an idiot. I turn around to say something to Rainie, but she's already gone. Great. Now Match and Harm have each other, and I'm back to being alone. Annoying.

I decide to attend afternoon storytelling with Ben, hoping it will provide some needed distraction. Ben is seated on one of the picnic tables on the lawn, with his feet resting on the bench. He is a tall man with a handlebar mustache and a pot belly. He's wearing a white tee shirt that has seen better days, carpenter's pants, and red suspenders. In a cardboard box next to him, I spot a couple of plastic light sabers and a Darth Vader mask.

Ben stands and steps up on top of the table. The crowd of campers falls silent. With no introduction, he starts to hum the theme to Star Wars. He gestures to the crowd to join in. Once there is a critical mass of humming, he begins to speak: "A long time ago in a galaxy far, far away …"

Ben is amazing. In about two hours, he performs the entire Star Wars trilogy—the original one—inviting people to stand up and play parts opposite him as he goes along. I'm shy at first, but, eventually, I agree to jump in as Leia in the third movie, making sure that Rainie sees how much fun I'm having, speeding across the moon of Endor.

At last, it is 4:30, and my mom arrives to rescue me. I have survived my first day of Fluidity camp.

No thanks to Rainie.

15

At home, I'm preparing to stomp off to my room for a good sulk, when Matty runs at me with a blanket and yells, "Buwwito fight!"

"Burrito fight" is a game the boys and I invented. It started out as "baby burrito," where I would wrap Matty in a blanket like a little burrito, then kiss his face and neck while his arms and legs were trapped. He would shriek with laughter and squirm around until he broke free. Then he'd say, "Do it again, Ceweste!" Soon enough, Devon wanted in on the action. Only he put his own spin on it, which is to say, instead of kissing, Devon would pelt the defenseless burrito with couch pillows. Turns out, Matty liked this just as much. And since "baby burrito" didn't seem to capture the spirit of the game anymore, we started calling it "burrito fight."

Now, I jump into the game, allowing Matty and Devon to wrap me up and sending them into fits of laughter with my threats to exact a pillowy revenge once I'm free. We manage to do a few rounds of this before dinner. Devon is definitely the master. He gets out of that swaddle faster than Houdini.

All the conversation at dinner is about Layla's swim trials. How fast she was. How she beat her personal best. How if she keeps this up, she will break every record known to man. I have almost completely tuned out, when my mom says, "Tell us about your first day, Celeste. Any highlights?"

"Um, it was okay, I guess."

"Was it weird?" asks Layla. "Did they make you drink goat's milk?"

"Layla!" says my mom. "That's not helpful."

"No," I say. "I didn't drink any goat's milk. Anyway, it wasn't that bad. The chanting was kind of cool." My mom looks at me like she wants to reach over and take my temperature.

Airhead says, "Chanting? That does sound cool. What was it like?"

"Well," I say, "you just sort of say these three sounds, all together ... I don't know, it's stupid."

"I don't think it's stupid," says Airhead, "I think we should try it. Can you show us?"

"I think that's a great idea," says my mom, beaming at Airhead like she just announced that she found the cure for cancer.

"Really? You want to try it?" I ask. "Okay. First we all hold hands." Everyone complies, even Devon. Okay. Good start. This could be cool. "Then we say, Om Ah Hung, all together, only you say each one really slowly. Ready?"

I start, "Oooooooom," and everyone joins in, one by one. It's working. Our voices start to blend together, vibrating at one frequency. Then, suddenly,

Layla bursts out laughing, which makes Devon laugh, then Matty. My mom and Airhead try to shush them, but it's too late.

I drop their hands and run upstairs. I make it to my room before I start crying. This time it's Layla who comes up to see me.

"Hey, Celeste, can I come in?"

"I guess."

She walks over to the bed and sits down, absent-mindedly holding her hand out over Rover, sprinkling his leaves with water.

"I'm sorry I laughed," she says. It wasn't on purpose, I swear."

"It's okay," I say. "I know you didn't mean to."

"Guess what? You know I beat my personal best at the trials today—"

"Yeah. So I heard."

"Well, I might get to try out for All Stars this fall."

"I thought you had to be a senior to do that."

"Me too. But that's what Coach said. It would mean more practices though."

"Oh."

"What was it like carpooling with the Langfords today? Was Rainie in one of her getups?"

"Not really. Did you know there are no rules there? You just kind of wander around and do whatever you feel like. As long as you do your job and show up for lunch, no one cares if you lie around in the grass the rest of the day. They call it self-exploration."

"Wow. I can't remember the last time I just sat in the grass. Or even just sat in one place, period. I'm always in the pool, in the car, in class, back in the pool. It's a little tiring sometimes."

Layla pauses for a moment, considering what she is about to say next. "Does Harm go to camp?"

"Harm?"

"Yeah, you know, Rainie's brother. I just wondered if he went to camp there too. I know he goes to DFS during the year, but I wasn't sure about the summer."

"Uh, I guess he goes to Fluidity. He rode there with us in the car. And I saw him at lunch."

"You rode with him? What was he like? Did you talk to him?"

"Layla, what is with you? Since when are you so interested in Harm Langford?"

"I'm not *interested* … I'm just … curious."

"Oh my God! You totally like him!"

"Shhhh. Not so loud. You don't have to broadcast it."

"Since when did this happen? Where have I been?"

"I didn't say anything because it's stupid. I haven't even talked to him in years. But have you seen him lately? He is SO cute now, with that black hair and those green eyes." Yeah, I've seen it. Rainie has that same black hair and green eyes. The combination is hard to miss.

"He is kind of cute, I guess. Do you want me to talk to him for you?"

"Oh my God, no! I would die of embarrassment. Just, maybe, find out if he has a girlfriend … if it comes up."

"You are so gone, it's not even funny. Okay, I'll do it. But you owe me."

"If you find that out, I will fold your laundry for a month!" She pauses and starts to frown. "Unless he actually has a girlfriend. Then I'll be devastated, and you'll have to cheer me up by folding my laundry for a month."

"Oh, no! I'm just the messenger here. Since when do I have to do your chores to make up for Harm having a girlfriend? Maybe I should just walk over there right now and tell him how you feel. Honesty really is the best policy." I pretend to get up off the bed and head for the door. Layla starts screaming and tackles me. Soon we are lying in a ball on the floor, laughing. My mom's head appears above us.

"Glad you two made up." She smiles. "Now come downstairs and finish your dinner."

16

It's the morning of day two. My mom has promised to drive me to camp, so one of the other swim parents picks Layla up before breakfast to take her to morning practice. Airhead and the boys are next. Airhead apologizes to my mom for leaving the kitchen in its usual state of post-breakfast chaos. My mom says it's no problem. Apparently, she is not bothered by having to scrape other people's soggy Cheerios and scrambled egg bits off the floor.

The boys take forever to get ready. By about the fiftieth time Airhead yells at Devon to brush his teeth and put his shoes on, I have come to terms with the fact that they may, in fact, never make it out the door. Finally, under threat of no TV, Devon relents and puts on his sneakers. The teeth, it seems, will have to wait. Airhead, one; Devon, one.

Now it's just me and my mom. Finally.

Ladies and Gentlemen, may I present, Act One of "Celeste Doesn't Want to Go to Camp."

I'm sitting at the kitchen table with a plate of scrambled eggs in front of me. I push them around the plate with my fork despondently.

"Is everything okay, sweetie?"

"Mmm."

"What's the matter?"

"I'm just not hungry."

Pout. More fork pushing.

"Do you feel okay?"

"Mmm."

"Did something happen yesterday?"

"No, I just don't feel well."

She puts her hands on my cheeks and forehead.

"Well, you don't feel hot. Are you sure it's not something to do with camp?"

My dilemma: if I fake illness, I will end up at the doctor's office, and my fraud will be exposed, but at least I will have escaped one day of camp. On the other hand, if I come clean and tell her that I don't want to go because I hate it there, she may take pity on me and let me stay home. Or she will tell me to suck it up and get in the car.

I decide to take my chances with the truth.

"Mom, please don't make me go back there. It's awful. I don't have any friends there."

"What about Rainie?"

"Maybe you haven't noticed, but Rainie and I haven't exactly been best buddies lately."

"I know you don't hang out all the time the way you used to, but that's why this summer is such a great opportunity—"

"It's not a 'great' anything. It sucks—"

Oops. She hates the word "sucks."

"Celeste, you've been there for one day. You told me you would give this a chance. Now, get your stuff together, and let's get in the car."

Argh. Blew it. Now I will have to wait at least a week before I try this again.

17

By the time we arrive, morning meeting has already begun. I say good-bye to my mom at the car and wander slowly along the path to the meeting house. The silence is punctuated by an occasional bird's song, or the bleating of a goat. Someone has left a canoe tied to the dock at the edge of the pond. The canoe fumbles around in the water, straining against its leash and adding a hollow percussion to the sounds of the morning as it bangs up against the dock. I stop for a moment to savor the feeling of the breeze swirling around me. The sun is slowly winning its battle with the morning mist. The pond is almost too bright to look at.

This place is kind of nice with no people in it.

When I get to the meeting house, I slip in the door and take a place at the edge of the circle. I see Rainie across the room. She is sitting with Harm and Match. Match spots me and nods. Rainie rolls her eyes and looks away. I decide to study my shoelaces. After the

"Om, Ah, Hung," I hightail it to the door and head directly to the Contribution Chart. Library, it says.

Phew. Books, I can handle.

It turns out that Ben, in addition to being the camp storyteller, is also the librarian. He welcomes me in with his mustached smile. We spend an hour or so in relative silence, re-shelving the books from the day before. Then he releases me. Another day of aimless self-exploration looms ahead of me.

I decide to weed the garden, even though it's not officially my job. I strip down to shorts and a tank top, crawling through the dirt, talking to the plants as I go. Forget hands and feet. My arms, legs, knees, and elbows plow through the dirt.

You can't get more in touch with the earth than this.

I apologize to the weeds for pulling them, assuring them that it is for the greater good. And I sing to the vegetables, trying to make selections that might interest them. The squash seem particularly fond of "You Are My Sunshine," so I decide to double up on that one.

Suddenly, from behind me, I hear a deep voice, echoing my words in perfect harmony. Match. I turn to him and smile. I take it to the chorus.

At some point, Match breaks off from his harmonies and interjects with a rap solo, which I can only assume he is making up as he goes along. You wouldn't know it from listening to him.

Sun's hot. Sweat drops.
She drags her feet through the filthy plot.
Now she's givin' it all she got.
She's not to be stopped. Got to be propped up.

Mud on her knees. Begs, borrows and pleads.
True Meadow song. So long in the face.
Wrong time, wrong place to be out of the source race.
No escape plan. Catching as catch can.
Row after row spans as weeds make their last stand.
Did I offend? Then why won't them plants bend?

Now, I'm not singing anymore. Just staring. Am I that obvious?

"That was amazing," I say, finally. "How did you do that?"

"It's mostly about breath control—"

"Right. But, how did you know what I was doing? I mean, *why* I was—"

"You're doing what we're all doing."

Still staring. Mouth still open. Match breaks the silence.

"I'm headed to the field to see if there's an ultimate game happening or something. You?"

"Um, maybe. Do you know what time it is?"

"Nah."

"I better head over to the pond and see if yoga is starting."

"Yoga?"

"You should try it."

"Not a chance. I'd rather drink goat's milk."

"Okay then."

"Catch you later."

With that he heads off over the hill.

Hunh. Maybe I have a friend here after all. A quiet, yet intimidating friend, who prefers ultimate to yoga, but still. That seems like progress.

Without having to speak about it, Match and I start showing up at the same time each morning to weed the garden. I crawl through the dirt, singing my little heart out, and he joins in, harmonizing, or adding a beat or a rap solo to spice up my act a bit. The best part, and the worst part, is that none of the other campers seem to pay much attention to what we are doing. I mean, when there are people wheeling around on unicycles, sitting in massage circles, and doing tai chi on the lawn, a couple of lunatics singing in the dirt doesn't seem to stand out so much.

Yoga with Shanti is my favorite part of the day. I'm near people, but I'm not forced to talk to them. I can let go of all my thoughts and just follow the sound of her voice. Even in the short time I've been here, I can see improvement in myself. Poses that used to make my muscles scream now provide a satisfying stretch. And my legs hardly shake at all in those extreme lunges Shanti seems to love so much. I look forward to Ben's storytelling, too. I know I can count on him to get a laugh out of me at each performance. Most of the time, though, I'm alone. Rainie and I succeed in avoiding each other, for the most part. Although for someone who wants nothing to do with me, she sure stares at me a lot. Of course, I only know this because I can't help staring at her, too.

18

Thursday night is the dreaded council meeting. Airhead has arranged for the boys to be at their other mom's house for the night, so that means my mom, Airhead, Layla, and I are off to see democracy in action. Oh, joy.

The town hall is the oldest building in Darwin. The stone steps dip in the middle from a century of wear and tear. The big copper dome on the top is green with age. Inside, the lobby opens up all the way to the domed ceiling. With all the people milling around on the marble floor, talking while they wait for the council meeting to start, the echo is deafening. I can't hear myself think. My mom looks similarly bothered. She gestures Jackie toward the door to the council chamber.

Thankfully, the chamber is carpeted. A center aisle leads up to a raised platform where the council members will sit. There is a microphone set up at the end of the aisle for people to address the council. The rest of the room is filled with rows of folding chairs. We take a seat a few rows from the back.

My mom and Airhead are chatting, and Layla is absorbed in her cell phone, so I alternate between staring into space and studying a copy of the meeting agenda, which I found waiting for me on my seat. Why, oh why, did I have to pick tonight to forget my phone at home?

I note with relief that zoning is first on the agenda, followed by budget, and then public works. Something in budget catches my eye: *Elizabeth Whitmore, Director of Fluidity School, Funding Request for Educational Pilot Program.*

"Mom," I whisper, tugging at her sleeve. "Mom, what's this?"

"Hmm?" She looks where I'm pointing on the agenda. "Oh. Isn't that interesting? Jackie, look. Fluidity is making a proposal tonight. We should stay for it."

Airhead nods without looking. "It's starting." she says.

The council members come out and take their seats. By their nameplates, I see that the center seat belongs to Myrna Braddock, a middle-aged woman with a chin-length brown bob and wire-rimmed glasses. The Earth and Air members are to her right, Fire and Water to the left. She bends the microphone toward her face and smiles out at the crowd. "All right. If you would all just take your seats, we are about to begin. As you know, I'm Open Seat Member, Myrna Braddock, and I will be moderating tonight's proceedings. We have a packed agenda tonight, so without further ado, let's begin with the permit applications. Could the applicants please line up at the microphone ... yes, that will speed things along. Thank you."

Airhead goes up to join the line. She is the last of four people. The first few go pretty quickly. One of them wants a shed, another needs a permit to put a second-floor addition over his garage. They all seem to be passing unanimously. Myrna opposes the third person's request to remove a two-hundred-year-old oak tree from his front lawn, but after his contractor comes up to testify that the tree roots are doing structural damage to the house, the other council members outvote her, and he gets his permit, too. Finally, it's our turn.

Airhead begins her presentation. It's a speech I have been hearing her practice all week ... daughter who's a swimmer ... young son following in her footsteps ... traveling back and forth to the Ocean Center is a burden ... need a full-sized pool for her to do proper laps ... blah blah blah.

Myrna breaks in, "Have you studied the environmental impact of your plan?"

Airhead looks confused. "Studied the environmental impact? No. It's a backyard pool."

"It's a backyard pool that is going to have spillage and, heaven forbid, leakage, which will introduce an unknown amount of saltwater into your backyard ecosystem."

"With all due respect," Airhead says, "there are several pools of this type already in the neighborhood. The only reason we need your permission is the setback. It's just six inches. I have asked all of our neighbors to sign, saying they have no objection, if you look at page four of the application—"

"I think you'll find, Ms. Neiman, that it is indeed within the purview of this council to consider the environmental impact of any proposal—"

The Air Party member, Gwendolyn Burr, breaks in, "Myrna, if I may, I think we've all had a chance to look over Ms. Neiman's application. At this point, I would move for a vote."

"Very well," says a reluctant Myrna. "All in favor?" The Air, Fire, and Water members raise their hands. "All opposed?" Myrna and the other Earth party member indicate their opposition. "The application has been approved."

My mom squeezes my hand. I poke Layla, who looks up from her phone.

"We got it," I say.

"Nice!" she says. "Wait 'til I tell Steph." And she goes back to her texting.

Airhead squeezes back into our row. She sits down next to my mom.

"Could you see me shaking up there?" she whispers.

"Not at all." my mom says. "You were great."

"Do you believe that woman?" Airhead mutters.

"Relax," says my mom. "You won, remember?"

"Oh, yeah." She smiles. "Remind me to send Gwen some flowers, would you?"

"Oh, look, Celeste, it's your camp director and ... who's that with her?"

I look up at the microphone, and there is Liz, flanked by an elderly black woman and ... Match.

"Match? What's he doing here?" I say.

"Who?" says my mom.

"Match is that friend she's been weeding with at camp," says Airhead. How does she know that? I only told my mom that. Whatever.

"Oh, I guess, I wasn't picturing him so ... tall," says my mom. "He's quite handsome. You never said how attractive he was."

"Ewww, Mom, could you not comment on how good looking my friends are? It's weird. I just don't understand what he's doing here."

Liz gestures to the elderly woman to take a seat in the front row. Match is chatting and playing around with a boy and girl, both about my age, also seated in the front row. The boy could be a carbon copy of him ... minus the tattoos.

Myrna bangs the gavel.

"All right, everyone. Let's come to order. Moving along to our budget agenda. Ms. Whitmore, I understand that you are here with a funding request on behalf of Fluidity School?"

"Well, that's not quite right," says Liz. "I'm here to request funding for an independent pilot program that we are proposing to run out of the Fluidity School. The money would go to the program, not to the school."

"Very well. Could you take us through the proposal?"

"Yes, of course. I know that you are all no doubt aware of the new census data that was released this past January by the governor. Our own neighboring City of New Preston has the largest concentration of unidentified citizens in the state and that percentage is growing every year. The latest census data shows that inner city youth are identifying later and later in life, some not at all. There is, of course, speculation as to why this is so. Pollution ... a diet of processed foods ... limited contact with organic environments. The point is, whatever the cause, we can help. Studies have shown that elementary and middle school children who participate in the suburban busing program are five times more likely than their peers to identify by the age of fifteen. And yet, we discontinue the busing right at the age when they need it most. That is, if they are lucky enough to get into the program in the first place."

Myrna glances down at her watch. Liz notices, but she soldiers on. "I don't ... I'm not sure if I'm making sense, here. What our program would do, is to sponsor unidentified inner city teens to attend high school at Fluidity, to offer them source counseling, provide them with homemade organic meals, exposure to a natural environment—"

"I'm sorry," Myrna breaks in, "that is all well and good, but isn't this a proposal you should be making to the New Preston City Council? Why is it that you think it would be appropriate for Darwin to fund this experiment?"

"Experiment? ... I ... this is not just an issue for the city. This is a community-wide issue. Perhaps if I could put a face on it. I'd like to introduce you to the first member of our pilot program, Tyrone Robbins." Match stands up and nods. All eyes on him, he takes his place next to Liz at the microphone.

"Hello, ma'am. I'm Tyrone Robbins. I live in southeast New Preston. I'm sixteen years old, and before I met Liz, I had to drop out of school because I'm unidentified, or partly identified, or something. All my friends call me Matchstick because of my one Fire finger." He holds up his hand and lights his index finger. "I have the Fire," he says, "but not the immunity, not all over, anyway. Sometimes I lay down wrong on my hand, and I wake up with my skin burning …" He gestures to the scars on his neck with his flaming finger and looks ready to make a new one when Myrna raises her hand.

"Okay, thank you, young man, that won't be necessary," says Myrna.

"It's not just me," says Match. "My brother and sister have nowhere to go to school next year."

Liz jumps back into the fray. "Tyrone and his siblings have lived in the Meadow neighborhood of New Preston their whole lives. Although we don't know for sure what has inhibited their development, this program gives them a fighting chance."

"Ms. Whitmore, your plea is not falling on deaf ears. The state of affairs in that neighborhood is appalling. No one would deny it. But you need to make your case before the City Council, not us. I move for a vote. All in favor?" No one on the council raises a hand. "All opposed?" Five hands. "Your request has been denied. Thank you, Ms. Whitmore. Thank you, young man."

There is murmuring among the crowd as Liz and Match go back to their seats. Airhead gestures to my mom, "C'mon. Let's slip out before the next presentation starts."

"Good idea. Celeste, do you want to go say 'hi' to your friend?"

"Um, no, that's okay. I think we should just go."

In the car, my mom turns to talk to me.

"Your friend has an incredible story. I wish I had known about that proposal sooner. We could've tried to help out."

"Don't look at me," I say. "I had absolutely no idea."

Airhead chimes in, "I wonder if Liz will take her proposal to New Preston. It sounds like a wonderful program. I'd hate to see it fail because they can't get the funding."

"I'm going to get in touch with Liz," my mom says. "There must be something we can do. I don't know, we could do some private fundraising, try to get it done that way."

"What about Dennis?" Airhead asks.

My dad?

"You know I can't ask him that. He'll just laugh it off as another one of my causes. Besides, you haven't seen my fundraising skills in action," she says, smiling.

"I can only imagine," says Airhead.

That night, I can't stop thinking about Match. How come I didn't know he had a brother and sister? Why didn't he tell me he was part of some pilot program? I guess I never asked.

* * *

The next morning, I show up for weeding, and Match is there, as usual.

"Hey," I say. Here goes nothing. "How was your night last night?"

"Okay," he says. "You?"

"Okay."

Well, so much for my conversation starter. I guess if he doesn't want to talk about it, it's none of my business. Conversation is overrated sometimes, anyway. I kneel down in the dirt and start in on the first few notes of "Dock of the Bay." Match's favorite. He smiles and joins in.

19

This weekend is a Darwin weekend for me and my sister, which means we don't go to our dad's overnight. Instead, we just have dinner with him at a restaurant on Friday night. This week it's Thai. I'm poking my fork around aimlessly in my mango chicken—usually, my favorite—when my dad takes the plunge and asks, "Everything okay, Celeste?"

"Dad, have you ever been to the Meadow?"

"I've driven through it before. Why do you ask?"

"A friend of mine from school lives there."

"Someone from the bus program?"

"No, sorry, I don't mean school. I mean camp. A friend of mine from Fluidity. He's part of a new program they're starting for high school kids."

"Oh, I wasn't aware of that."

Layla says, "You mean the guy who was at the council meeting?"

"Yeah. His name's Match. I mean, Tyrone."

Layla breaks in, "Dad, you should have seen him. He has scars all over from burning himself with this one Fire finger—"

Now it's my turn to interrupt. "The *point* is he's part of this new program for unidentified teens to come to Fluidity. The natural environment is supposed to help them, you know, bring out their source. The only thing is, they need money. Match has a brother and sister, who don't have anywhere to go to school next year. Plus, there could be hundreds of other kids like them, or even thousands, or something."

My dad isn't one to beat around the bush.

"What are you asking me, Celeste?"

"Well, I thought, maybe, you could help."

"How much money are we talking about?"

"Um. I'm not sure. What does a year at Fluidity cost?"

"A year of tuition at Fluidity School costs $23,000," he says without hesitation. "And that doesn't include fees, books, and supplies."

"What? No way! That's insane!" says Layla.

"I wasn't going to use exactly those words, but your sister's right, Celeste. That's an awful lot of money to give to a program I know nothing about. Is there any research behind what they're trying to do? I'll tell you what. You do the research and come to me with a real proposal. Then we'll talk."

Okay. At least that's not a straight out "no." I guess I have some more research to do.

Saturday morning comes, and the whole family is getting ready to go to the Ocean Center to watch one of Layla's meets. I beg off, promising my mom that I won't spend the whole morning watching TV while they are gone. I never said I wouldn't use the computer though.

Once I have the house to myself, I run up to my mom and Airhead's room and log on. This time I search for "unidentified + Meadow." Over five thousand results. One study says that there are over two million unidentified people in New Preston, which is a city of about eight million people. Of that two million, a startling thirty-five percent live in the historically black and impoverished "Meadow" neighborhood, despite the fact that the neighborhood makes up only eighteen percent of the city's population.

Wow. If my math is right (and there's no guarantee of that), then that means about one of every two people in the Meadow is unidentified. Half? Compare that to one in five for the rest of New Preston. And even that seems high. I search for the national average. One in ten. Wow. That can't just be because unidentified people tend to move to urban areas, like I've been told. People aren't moving to the Meadow.

I try a few more searches for studies about unidentified + cities, unidentified + natural environments, unidentified + whatever I can think of. Unfortunately, I'm not finding anything useful. There are plenty of statistics about high rates of unidentification in cities, but not much about what might be causing it.

After a while, I give up and go watch TV. Anyway, it's not like I watched TV the whole time they were gone.

20

By Monday morning of my second week at
Fluidity, I'm just about sure that I can make it
through a whole summer of this—weed, swim, yoga,
repeat—when I find out my job for the day. Milk the
goats.

Oh, no. No. No, no, no. Just, no.

I look behind me, and Rainie is standing there,
studying me. She reads the panic on my face. I look
back at her with my best impression of a baby deer in
headlights. "Okay, relax, Swergie," she says. "I'm on
it."

"Swergie?" I say. "No one's called me that in
years."

"Yeah? That's because I'm the one who made it
up, and you haven't talked to me in years."

Fair enough.

She looks over at one of the girls next to us.
"Hope, will you switch with Celeste today? She's new.
I want her on dishes with me."

"Sure," says Hope. "I had it three times last week. She can have a turn."

I lean over to Rainie and whisper, "Dishes? Are you sure? Wouldn't weeding or something be better?"

She whispers back, "Just trust me."

Trust her? Well, why not? It's not like I have many options here.

"Okay," I say. "Dishes it is."

After that, I join Rainie for watercolors down by the pond, then convince her to do yoga with me in the pavilion. If you've never seen Rainie Langford try to do Warrior Three pose, you haven't lived. It's hysterical.

The cow bell rings, and we head for the dining hall. Without a word being spoken about it, I join Rainie's table for lunch. As usual, Match and Harm are holding court with a group of Fluidity girls, who laugh insipidly at every word they say.

Things get a little heated between Harm and Rainie when Harm suggests that he knows the best way to make a Mohawk stand up. He says, tease it and douse it with a can of hair spray. She says, Elmer's glue. I really think the fight's about to get physical, when Match starts laughing and tells us we should all just shave our heads. Before I know it, Rainie and I are headed into the kitchen for cleanup.

"Hi, Nona," says Rainie, greeting a tall, thin woman with a long, gray braid, who is busy stacking dishes by the sink. "This is Celeste. She's on dishes with us today."

"Hey, Celeste. Welcome. What do you think, girls? Billy Joel? Shakira?" She has moved over to the end of the counter, and she is flipping through a travel case of CDs.

"Got any Blondie?" asks Rainie, winking at me.

"Nope. Sorry, Rainie."

"What about *The Big Chill?*" asks Rainie. "Since it's her first time and all."

"True, that is how it all began," says Nona. "Not that you two are old enough to have seen that movie—"

"Please, I saw it ages ago," says Rainie. "My parents can't stop watching it. They own it." She looks over at me. "There's this scene where they all dance around and clean up the kitchen to the Temptations. That's where Nona got the idea for musically-assisted clean-up. She's been doing it ever since."

"All right then," says Nona. "Let's stop yapping and get to it."

She sticks in a CD, presses a few buttons, and soon the room fills with the sounds of "Ain't Too Proud to Beg."

Nona and Rainie start to dance around the kitchen, putting away food and putting dirty dishes in the sink, stopping occasionally to swing each other around or smash their hips together on the way by. Nona begins to wash the dishes, while Rainie feeds her more dirty ones from the stack. Rainie tosses me a dish towel and gestures toward the growing pile of clean plates.

For a minute I just stand there, but they are both gesturing at me … and it does look kind of fun. Before I can talk myself out of it, I'm waving the towel around my head and twirling my way toward the counter. Okay, I can see where this beats yanking weeds out of the dirt.

That night at dinner, I still can't get the Temptations song out of my head. I'm absent-mindedly humming and eating my food when I look up to see everyone staring at me. Everyone but Devon. He's too busy trying to set his carrots on fire.

Geez, you'd think I never had a good day before.

When I crawl into bed that night, I take Rover into my lap and gently brush the dust off his leaves. I'm singing him a few rounds of "This Land is Your Land" when my mom pokes her head in my door.

"Hi sweetie, I don't mean to interrupt." She looks at the plant in my lap. If she's thinking something about it, she doesn't say it. "I just wanted to say good night."

"Good night, mom," I say. "I love you."

"I love you too, sweetie." She smiles and shuts the door. I put Rover back on the side table. "I love you, too, Rover," I say. Nothing. Not even a twitch. Come on, already! What does a girl have to do to get a little plant love around here?

21

Rainie and I start to hang out together whenever we can, which, at Fluidity, is all the time. We work it out so our jobs are together. With Rainie's help, I even feed the goats. I still have no plans to milk them anytime soon, but I manage to get food in their trough without getting kicked, bitten, or peed on, so I consider my efforts at goat care a fabulous success. Raja even has a little crush on me. Either that or he thinks my ponytail is breakfast. Whatever it is, he won't stop nuzzling me, which would be cute, if his mouth weren't so disgusting.

I haven't done my morning weeding in a while, but if Match has noticed, he hasn't said anything. I still see Match every day at lunch. Match, Harm, Rainie, and I always sit at the same table. Rainie and I entertain ourselves by watching the Fluidity girls throw themselves at Harm and Match. I'd never really noticed it before, but there aren't that many boys at Fluidity. And the ones that *are* there? Let's just say, they are not exactly makeout material. That leaves our two resident hunks with the pick of the litter, you might say.

So far, neither of them seems that interested any of the Fluidity girls, which is good news for Layla. Unless, of course, Harm has a girlfriend from somewhere else that I don't know about.

Friday at lunch, I see an opportunity, and I take it. Layla's swim team will be competing in a regional meet at the Olympic Sea Dome in New Preston on Sunday, and I figure that tempting the guys with a look inside the Sea Dome is as good a way as any to get Layla on Harm's radar screen. I ask Match, Rainie, and Harm if they want to meet me there. No surprise, the boys jump at it. Slightly more of a surprise, Rainie does, too. She seems excited, even.

I feel good. I have plans. I have friends. Only now do I realize just how lonely I have been the past couple of weeks. The only problem is, the days are slipping by, and I'm no closer to finding out my source than when school ended. All of my weeding and singing and poetry reading has gotten me nowhere. And I'm not even doing much of that anymore. Spending time with Rainie has distracted my focus.

On Friday night, Layla and I go to our dad's for the weekend. He lives in a totally decked-out apartment in New Preston, and I love going there. Most of our time with our dad is spent exploring the city, taking walks to parks, museums, shops. Plus, my cat, Pumpkin, is there. He's orange and fat, obviously. He's also a warm, furry ball of love. I miss his purry perfectness when I'm not there.

We are having takeout Indian food tonight. Chicken tikka masala, lamb vindaloo, channa saag, and garlic naan. And don't forget the mango lassis. I pour mine into one of my dad's martini glasses and sip it with a straw. The height of sophistication.

"Who's the favorite this weekend?" my dad asks Layla, as he spoons rice onto his plate.

"North New Preston, as usual," says my sister with a pout. "Dana Cummings broke the junior world record two weeks ago."

"Don't worry about her," my dad says, "just focus on setting your own personal record. Everyone else is just window dressing. It worked for me."

"I know, I know," she says. "That's what Coach says, too. It's just so hard. No matter what I do, it seems like she's always just ahead of me."

"Well, he told me you cut a half a second off your fifty freestyle since the spring. You've been working on rotating your elbows more, haven't you?"

She smiles. "Yeah. That was good advice. Thanks, Dad."

He turns his attention to me. "And you, young lady. Any thoughts about what you might like for your birthday this year? Fourteen is a big one."

Is it? I hadn't noticed.

"I don't know. It's no big deal, really."

"No big deal? My little girl is going to high school. It sounds like a big deal to me. If you don't ask for anything, I'll just pick something out myself, and I don't think anyone would be happy about that."

"True. I still have nightmares about that dress you picked out for me when I was twelve." I fake a shudder.

"I know," he says. "What about a trip to Paris, for the three of us?"

Now we're talking.

"Paris, really? Oh my God, Dad, that would be so cool!"

"I was thinking about the end of August. I'll ask your mom about it."

Layla and I look at each other in disbelief. Oh la la!

We finish our dinner—with a conspicuous lack of fireballs, slamming cabinet doors, and vegetable warfare—then watch a movie and head off to bed. I corner Layla at the sink while she is brushing her teeth.

"I like my shirts folded so that I can see the design on the front, like they do at the mall."

She spits toothpaste into the sink.

"Did you just hit your head on something? Why would I care how you fold your shirts?"

"Oh, I don't know, maybe because I asked Rainie, Match, and Harm to come to your meet on Sunday, and they said 'yes'?"

"Oh my God, seriously? Wait, you didn't say it was my idea, did you?"

"No, of course not."

"Oh my God, Celeste. You are a genius! Oh my God, Oh my God, okay, I have to tell Gina … and Kim … and Stephanie. Celeste, you are the best!"

She kisses me on the cheek, grabs her cell phone from the bathroom counter and starts tapping away.

"Yeah, yeah, just remember, mall-style!"

I leave her to her texting and head down the hall to my room.

In my dreams that night, I'm backstage at my school's auditorium, about to go on. But what play is it? Quick, what are my lines? I look around to see what everyone else is doing. They all seem to know where to go and what to say. I can't even tell what kind of costume I have on. Am I supposed to sing? What is my cue? Somebody, tell me! Too late, I have to go on, I have to ... OUCH!

Pumpkin lets out a blood-curdling yowl, and I realize I'm lying directly on top of him. "Sorry, P-kins," I whisper. Apparently, he does not accept my apology because the minute I roll off him, he shoots off the bed and scampers out of the room. No way I can go back to sleep now.

It's not even 8:00 a.m. yet, and my dad and Layla like to sleep in, so I have a couple of hours to kill on my own. I pour myself a bowl of cereal and sit down at my dad's computer. No password protection. Awesome.

This time I search for "how to bring out your source." Four hundred thirty-six thousand results. Whoa. Someone called SourceSeeker1736 has posted a question on *Yahoo! Answers*: "Is there a natural way to bring out your source? I have tried the hormone therapies and the prescription medications, and I can't stand the side effects. Help! There has to be something I can do!"

The response voted "best answer" by the most users comes from U4life: "I agree the hormone therapies are awful. A friend recently told me about the Source Cleanse diet. It's supposed to rid your body of toxins, so that your source can come out. I had my doubts at first, but it really works. Within a week of trying it, I had plants bending to me, and now I have officially identified as an Earth, at 28 years old! Guess I'll have to change my screen name. (: Try it! www.sourcecleanse.com."

I click the link and start to read. "Are you unidentified with nowhere to turn? Tired of medications that cost a fortune and don't deliver? Bring out your source the all natural way, at a fraction of the cost, with the Source Cleanse diet." All natural sounds good. A fraction of the cost also sounds good, considering I have no money.

"Source Cleanse is a blend of green tea, garlic, and other natural herbs and spices. Forty-eight hours of fasting and drinking only Source Cleanse has been proven to clear toxins from the body to create the ideal conditions for your source to surface." I browse the testimonials. Loads of happy customers. Terrific. What's the catch?

The catch is that the retail price for a liter of Source Cleanse is $24.99, and you're supposed to drink at least four liters during the forty-eight hour fast. Did I mention that I have no money? I search the Web to see if someone has posted a list of ingredients. A handful of people claim to have re-created Source Cleanse in their own kitchens. I choose the recipe with the fewest ingredients and print it out: green tea, garlic, agave syrup, ginger, and cayenne pepper. I'm sure we have all that stuff at my mom's house. I can make it on Sunday and start the fast after dinner. By the end of next week, I'll be signing up for source school.

Before I log off, I glance at a banner ad on the side of the screen. "U can be happy!" it says. The ad links to U-can-be-happy.org. I've heard of this before. It's an organization devoted to sending the message that people can be happy being a "U." The site has links to video clips of celebrities who talk about growing up unidentified and how it didn't stop them from reaching their dreams. I'm surprised to see a few of my favorite actors and actresses on the list. I listen to them tell their stories ... many of them were kicked out of source school, or quit when it became too hard to fake it anymore. Some left home and ended up living on the street. But, inevitably, they say, it was better than living a lie. They were true to themselves, and now they are happier for it. Not to mention rich and famous.

That's nothing like me, I think. I'm not planning to live a lie. Just the opposite. I'm trying to find out who I really am. I'm just being ... proactive about it.

I shut down the computer and take the list of the ingredients off the printer. I fold it up and hide it in the bottom of my backpack.

What? Having a little privacy is not the same as living a lie.

22

The Sea Dome is enormous. It makes the pool at the Ocean Center in Darwin look like a hot tub. The main racing tank runs down the center of the stadium, its thick glass walls rising twenty feet up from the cement floor. Bleachers line both of the long sides of the rectangular tank, so that spectators can have a fish's-eye view of the underwater contests. Huge tubes—underwater corridors, really—protrude from the short ends of the main tank, connecting it with a network of warming tanks, where the athletes immerse themselves and prepare for their races.

When my dad and Layla and I arrive, my mom and Airhead are already there, waiting near Layla's assigned warming tank. Devon and Matty aren't with them, so they must be at their other mom's for the day. My mom swoops in.

"Hello, Dennis. Hi, girls."

She gives me a quick kiss on the forehead, then turns her attention to Layla.

"How are you feeling, sweetie? Did you keep hydrated, yesterday?"

My mom walks with Layla to the mats where her teammates are stretching and preparing to submerge. That leaves me alone with dad and Airhead. Ugh.

Airhead says hello, but doesn't hug or kiss me. She never does when my dad is there. My dad is friendly enough to her, but it's pretty clear that he's drawn a line in the sand that she has decided not to cross. Their attempt at small talk is painful. Airhead comments that rain is in the forecast for the week. She hopes that it will clear up in time for the Fourth of July fair next weekend. My dad observes that no forecast beyond forty-eight hours has any scientific degree of reliability, so it's anyone's guess. I'm looking around desperately for an escape, when I see Match, Harm, and Rainie walking towards us. I have never been so relieved to see anyone in my life. And, from the look of it, I'm not the only one. Airhead looks over at my friends like a lost puppy who just found her way home.

"Rainie, Harm!" she yells, a little too loudly. She waves them over frantically.

"Hi, Ms. Neiman," say Harm and Rainie.

"Please, kids, call me Jackie. You're making me feel old," she says, giving them each a quick hug.

"Hi, Mr. Jardine," they say, waving in my dad's direction.

My dad says hello to Rainie and Harm, then turns his gaze to Match.

"Dad, Jackie, this is Tyrone. He's a friend from camp," I say. My dad shakes Match's hand.

"Nice to meet you, Tyrone," he says.

Airhead looks him up and down. "You must be the 'Match' we've heard so much about," she says, and she goes in for the hug.

So, to summarize, the only one Airhead has *not* hugged in this situation—besides my dad—is me, the one who is technically, legally related to her. Not that I want to be hugged by her. I'm just saying. I notice these things.

"We should go say 'hi' to Layla before she submerges," I say.

We walk over to the mats where Layla is stretching. She gets up and fidgets with her suit as we walk over. She rips off her swim cap and lets her blonde hair fall down around her shoulders. Subtle, she is not.

Then again, maybe subtlety is overrated, because Harm seems to be paying attention. As we approach, Harm struggles to keep his gaze at eye level, and if I'm not mistaken, the Romeo of Fluidity Camp is blushing. Rainie and I look at each other with a silent "are you seeing what I'm seeing?" Match, on the other hand, has other things to look at, like Layla's teammates stretching out in bathing suits all around us. You can thank me later, Match.

We barely have time to say hello before Layla's coach blows a whistle, causing the lounging swimmers to snap to attention and assemble at the base of the warming tank. Layla rushes to put her swim cap back on and joins the group. The swimmers climb the stairs and plunge into the water one by one, like lemmings off a cliff.

Instinctively, I run over to the side of the tank and watch as Layla descends into the salty water. The gills on her neck expand, and the skin between her fingers and toes fans out. She swims over to me and we peer at each other through the glass. For a moment, I have the odd sensation that my sister is an aquarium attraction, something that families with small children would pay money to see, but only when it's too cold outside to go to the park and play for free.

She looks at me expectantly, and I oblige with our little pre-race ritual. I cup my hands and hold them up to the sides of my neck, waving them back and forth like gills. Then I make the shape of a heart with my fingers and hold it up to the glass. She makes the same heart and presses it against the other side of the glass. "Good luck, Fishface," I mouth. She smiles.

Our ritual complete, Layla turns and begins to warm up inside the tank. She picks up speed as she circles the depths of the pool. She has yet to surface. She has no need. The sight of her swimming is beautiful, other-worldly. I realize that I have avoided going to see her compete for a long time, longer than I care to admit. Jealous much? Now, I can't take my eyes off her. And neither can Harm, I see. You go, Layla!

We make our way over to the bleachers as the first set of swimmers enters the main tank. They swim to their starting blocks. A series of underwater pulses signals the "ready, set, go," and they are off. This scenario repeats itself endlessly throughout the afternoon. The only excitement—if you want to call it that—is when Layla or one of her teammates is up, and we have someone to root for.

Match hangs in there for about an hour before he makes his excuses and heads for home. I don't blame him. That's longer than I would last if I weren't forced to be here. Harm and Rainie tough it out until the end with me though, and I'm grateful for that. Otherwise, I'd be stuck alone with my parents and Airhead, which is one of the more awkward configurations of our crazy, mix-and-match family.

I look over at my dad. I can see the faint lines of his dormant gills extend down from behind his ears toward the base of his neck. There is such pride in his eyes when he watches her race.

At one point, I'm so excited to tell Rainie about my birthday trip to France that I blurt it out in front of everyone. Big mistake. Apparently, my dad hadn't run the idea by my mom yet, so she gets all pissy about it, and I can tell they're gonna fight about it later.

In one of the final rounds, Layla comes head-to-head with her archrival, Dana Cummings. The good news is it's Layla's best event—the fifty freestyle. Layla already set a new personal record in one of the earlier rounds. She has the best time in this event so far today. When she enters the main tank, Layla searches the crowd and finally locks eyes with my dad. He smiles at her and nods. She gets into position with the other swimmers. Our entire group goes silent. No one even breathes.

The pulses break the silence, and the swimmers take off. Dana and Layla quickly break away from the pack. The race is so short, I barely scream her name before it is over. But what happened? I look around. Did anyone catch that? No one else seems to know either. We look to the scoreboard. After some anxious seconds, the rankings appear.

Layla is second to Dana, again. By two hundredths of a second. Yikes. I can see the disappointment in her eyes. My parents, on the other hand, don't exhibit one bit of disappointment. They are on their feet, clapping and screaming. The rest of us follow suit. Layla recovers quickly, congratulating Dana and swimming off to her warming tank.

At last, the meet comes to an end. We stretch our legs, stiff from over two hours on the metal benches, and wander back over to the warming tanks. My dad—never one to linger at these events—says his good-byes and walks over to blow Layla a kiss through the glass on his way out the door.

While the rest of us wait for Layla to resurface, Airhead looks at her watch nervously.

"I'm going to have to call Jen. The boys are due back at five. Unless we leave in the next ten minutes, we're not going to make it."

"I'm sorry," says my mom. "You were right. We should have brought two cars."

Harm sees an opportunity.

"I can drive Layla and Celeste home, Ms. Jardine."

"Oh, Harm, that's sweet," my mom says, "but I think I should wait for Layla. She still has to resurface and shower."

Airhead looks at Harm, then at me. I give her my best "please, make this happen" eyes. I have to give Airhead this much. Sometimes, she just gets it.

"What a great idea!" says Airhead. "You kids should all ride together. Thank you, Harm. That is really considerate."

My mom looks at her, annoyed. Unperturbed, Airhead grabs my mom's arm and says, "Come on, Lena. Let's go ask Layla what she would like to do."

Apparently, Layla approves of the idea, because by the time they get back, my mom has resigned herself to the situation.

"All right," says my mom, "You know your way out of here, Harm?"

"Yes, ma'am, the GPS was right on the money."

"Okay, then. If you need to, just call our cell phones. Do you have our numbers?"

I break in, "I have your numbers, mom. We'll be fine."

"Okay," she says. "Drive carefully. We'll see you at home."

"Bye, kids," says Airhead, and she drags my mom from the arena floor.

23

It's really hard not to laugh. So Rainie and I do laugh, crouched down in the backseat of the Langfords' car, watching our older siblings caught up in some kind of teenage mating ritual.

"You were really good," says Harm to Layla. "It's so cool the way you can ... do that."

"Thanks," she says. "Sorry it was so boring."

"It wasn't boring. It was really cool. I've never seen you swim before. I mean, anyone like you ... a Water, swim before."

"Well, I'm glad you liked it because it's all I ever do. I mean, not that you have to like what I do."

"I do ... like it. Can I come to another meet sometime?"

Her face lights up.

"Sure. I usually have one every weekend. Some of them are pretty far away though. I'll let you know the next time we have one nearby."

"Thanks."

"Um, what do you, like, do when you're not in school?"

"Do? I, uh, I've been working on my singe art. It's kind of like collage, but with some Fire techniques. I could show you some stuff I have in the garage."

"I'd like that."

I'd like that? Rainie and I play at imitating the happy couple for a while. I look at Rainie in feigned adoration, giggle, and bat my eyelashes. She slouches down, pretending to have one hand placed coolly on a steering wheel, giving me her best Harm-as-James-Dean. She fakes a yawn and reaches her free arm around my shoulders.

Soon, we bore of this, however, and we stop paying attention to the spectacle in the front seat. Instead, we tip our heads back and look out the windows silently, watching as the New Preston skyline slips away behind us. Rainie's arm is still stretched across the back seat. I rest my cheek on her forearm and fall asleep.

I don't wake up until we pull into the Langfords' driveway. I'm mortified to find my cheek plastered to Rainie's arm with a sticky patch of dried spit. As I pull away, it's like pulling a band-aid off my cheek. Rainie just laughs.

"Man, you were OUT," she says, rubbing her arm with the glove of her other hand.

We all get out of the car. I have a sudden urge to pee, so I thank Harm for the ride and say to Layla, "You coming?"

Layla blushes and says, "Um, Harm was going to show me some of his art. I'll be over in a minute."

"Okay, see you guys tomorrow."

"Bye," says Rainie. "See you tomorrow." She climbs the stairs to the porch and goes inside. I head across the street, looking back as Harm and Layla duck under the garage door.

Inside, Devon and Matty are parked in front of the TV, watching cartoons. Airhead and my mom are in the kitchen getting dinner ready.

"Hi, sweetie," says my mom. "You're back just in time to set the table," she says with a smile.

"Fantastic," I say.

"Where's Layla?" she asks.

"Um, she's ... looking at Harm's art," I say.

Airhead giggles and dumps some pasta into a pot of boiling water.

"Am I missing something?" says my mom.

"I hope so," says Airhead. "It's better that way."

Now I start to giggle.

"You two are impossible," she says, but she's smiling. "Celeste, can you go let your sister know that dinner will be ready in ten minutes?"

I go back out on the front porch. I'm about to walk down the stairs, when the motion sensor light on the Langfords' garage flashes on, and I see Harm and Layla ... kissing. Not just kissing. KISSING. Open-mouthed, I-want-to-swallow-you-whole, movie kissing.

Layla opens her eyes and sees me on the porch, staring at them. She taps Harm on the shoulder and he looks over at me, sheepishly.

"Dinner's almost ready," I shout, lamely, and go back inside.

My cheeks are still burning red as I finish setting the table. Airhead gives me a knowing look, which does nothing to put out the fire under my skin. Layla walks in, trying to act casual, but her cheeks are flushed pink, which, for a Water, is about as hot as they can be.

Layla and I both inhale our dinners, then sit there, tortured, while Matty has a standoff with Airhead about eating the four pieces of broccoli he is required to swallow before getting dessert. Finally, we are released. Layla and I immediately retreat to the third floor for a debriefing.

"What was that?" I say in mock surprise.

She is pink again.

"I can't believe you were watching us," she says. "What were you doing out there?"

"Me? Mom told me to go get you for dinner. You're lucky she didn't go get you herself. She seems to be suffering from some sort of blissful parental ignorance. Airhead is totally onto you, though. So, what happened?"

She tells me how they talked and talked the whole way home—as if I wasn't there—about her swimming, about DWS and DFS, about his decision not to go to Fluidity full time.

"Get to the kissing part already," I say impatiently.

Refresh the pink.

"I don't know how it happened. We came out of the garage. I started shivering, and he reached up and started rubbing my arms. His hands were so warm ... I think I told him that ... and then, he kissed me."

"What was it like?"

"It was like ... sticking my tongue in an electrical socket."

"Eww. Ouch."

"No, I mean, in a good way. My lips were buzzing, like electricity was running through them. I don't know how else to describe it."

"So, are you two, like, boyfriend and girlfriend now?"

"Uh, I don't know. He asked me to the fair this weekend. Oh my God! I have to tell Gina and Steph I'm not going with them anymore."

She grabs her phone, and I take the hint, heading back down to the second floor. Devon and Matty streak by me, stark naked and dripping with water. "Boys!" Airhead screams from the bathroom. "Slow down! You're going to fall and crack your heads open!"

I slip quietly into my room and sit down on the bed next to Rover. "Hey, Rove, did you miss me this weekend?" No response. "Okay, fine. Ignore me." I open my backpack and take out the Source Cleanse recipe. I glance at the clock. One hour since dinner. My fast has already begun.

24

Getting out the door Monday morning without eating breakfast is easy. I never really eat much in the mornings anyway, so no one notices. And I always bring a big water bottle to camp. It's just that this time, I fill it with my own homemade garlic tea. As I'd hoped, we had most of the ingredients lying around the kitchen. No fresh garlic or ginger, but I figure the powdered stuff will work just as well. The taste is, um, interesting. I put in some extra agave to make it go down easier.

By lunchtime, it has been about eighteen hours since my last meal, and I'm ready to pass out. Or bite somebody's head off. Or both. I sit next to Rainie in the dining hall and sip my tea. Match and Harm sit across from us, absorbed in their own conversation, as usual.

"Aren't you going to eat anything?" Rainie asks.

"I'm not that hungry," I lie. I look at the last few bites of Rainie's burrito sitting on the plate. Black beans, rice, cheese, salsa, and Nona's fresh guacamole. The saliva pools in my mouth.

"What is that you're drinking?" Rainie asks. "No offense, but it smells disgusting."

"It's tea," I say. "Talk to me again about disgusting smells in an hour after you've eaten that burrito."

"Geez, sorry, just asking. Why are you acting so weird?"

"I'm not acting weird. I'm just sitting here drinking my tea. Why are you acting weird?"

"I'm not. If you're not going to eat anything, let's get out of here. I'm done."

We leave the dining hall and walk down by the pond where the art supplies are. Just about everyone is still eating, so we have the place to ourselves. We each grab a sketchbook and sit down in the grass next to Willow.

"Are you going to the Fourth of July fair this weekend?" asks Rainie.

"Yeah, um, May's coming back from camp for the weekend, so we're gonna go together."

"Who's May?" she says, evenly.

"She's my best friend from school. She's at Camp Gray Rock this summer." I try not to sound as guilty as I feel.

"Oh. Sounds fancy." She's quiet. I know I should ask her to come with us, but the truth is, I haven't seen May in a long time, and I don't really want to have to explain Rainie to her. I just want to hang out with May and catch up.

"Yeah, anyway, I'd ask you to come, but May's parents are taking us, so …"

"Whatever. I can't go anyway. My parents are having this big barbecue thing I have to go to. I was going to see if you wanted to come."

"Oh. Well, I'm going to be at the fair, so ..."

"You could stop by after. It usually goes all night."

"Yeah, okay. Maybe I'll stop by when I get back."

"Maybe. Right."

The silence is awful. I pick the first thing I can think of to fill it. I tell Rainie about seeing Harm and Layla kissing in the driveway.

"I knew it!" she says. "I was all over Harm when he came in last night, but he wouldn't tell me a thing."

"I think Airhead knows. She kept giggling and giving me this look—"

"Why do you call her that?"

"What?"

"Airhead. Why do you call her that?"

"I don't know. It's just a nickname."

"Well, it's kind of mean. I mean, it makes me wonder what you've been saying about me behind my back all this time."

My pause is too long.

"Oh my God," says Rainie. "You have been saying things about me!"

"Oh, like you never said anything mean about me."

"Not once, and you know it!"

"Yeah? Well, maybe that's because you didn't have any friends to say it to." The minute it comes out of my mouth, I know I've gone too far.

"Rainie, I am SO sorry, I didn't mean that. I'm just so hungry ... Do you want to know why I'm not eating, and why I'm drinking this disgusting garlic water?"

"Please, do tell," she says.

"I looked up this website, and it said that if I drink this stuff and don't eat for two days, it'll help bring out my source. Instead, I'm just hungry and tired and annoyed. The whole thing is so stupid."

"Why do you care so much about that stuff?"

"I don't know. Why *don't* you? Don't you want to go to a normal school some day? Or do you want to be stuck at Fluidity your whole life?"

"For your information, I am not *stuck* here. I like it here. I thought you liked it, too, but you don't, do you? You're just stuck ... stuck-up is more like it. All you can think about is how to get into your stupid source school. Not everyone cares if they identify, you know. There is such a thing as just being ... I don't know, yourself—"

She is still talking, but I'm no longer listening to her. I'm just staring ... staring as smoke starts to pour out of her gloves.

"Rainie, are you okay? What's wrong with your hands?" She looks down at her hands, then back at me, and I know what her gloves have been hiding.

"Oh my God, Rainie, you're a Fire! How long have you known? How is that even possible?"

She jumps up. "I'm not! I'm not anything. And you better not go around saying that to anybody else. Just, just, mind your own business, and leave me alone!" I sit, in stunned silence, as she runs off toward the meeting house.

A group of kids has wandered down from the dining hall. They are sifting through the art supplies and chatting. This snaps me out of my state of shock.

I look down at the bottle of garlic water in my hand and dump it into the ground without a second thought. Forget the whole fasting thing. I'm going to need some serious junk food to help me process this tonight.

25

That night at dinner, I stuff my face with macaroni and cheese like there is no tomorrow. My mom definitely notices, but she doesn't say anything. After I'm excused from the table, I sneak a carton of ice cream from the freezer, grab a couple of spoons, and make the climb up to Layla's room.

"Can I come in?" I ask, peeking up over the edge of the attic stairwell. "I have ice cream."

She eyes the carton.

"Okay. Come on in. I guess a little bit wouldn't hurt."

We settle onto her bed with the ice cream between us.

Between spoonfuls, I manage, "I had a fight with Rainie today."

"Why, you couldn't decide whether to lie around doing yoga or lie around drawing pictures?"

"Whoa. Where did that come from?"

"Sorry, I'm just super tired. I have double practices all week, plus a meet on Sunday, and mom's threatening not to let me go to the fair with Harm Saturday night."

"What? Why not?"

"She wants me to be rested for the meet, I guess."

"What did you tell her?"

"I pretty much said that if she didn't let me go I wasn't going to swim on Sunday."

"Good for you."

"Yeah, she backed off. But she said I have to be home by nine, or else."

"Or else what?"

"I'm not sure. There's nothing in my life she doesn't control already. She thinks she can take Harm away from me, maybe?"

"That sucks, Layla. I'm so sorry."

"I know. What I really want to do is quit swim camp and come to Fluidity with you."

"You do? Are you insane? Why would you *want* to go there?"

"Um, think about it, Celeste. Why would I *want* to go somewhere where I could hang out with Harm all day?"

Oh, yeah.

"Well, I would trade places with you in a minute if I could. You are so lucky. You've been identified since you were eight. You've never had to worry about where you belong—"

"I never had a choice in the matter, did I? You want my life? Practices every morning at 5:30. Swim meets every weekend."

Hmm. Five-thirty does sound a bit early.

111

"Okay. I get your point. Just don't go thinking life is so wonderful at Fluidity all the time. We've all got problems, you know."

Somehow, during all of this, we have managed to finish the entire carton of ice cream.

"Oh my God," says Layla, "I cannot believe that I just ate all that. Coach would kill me if he found out!"

"Your coach cares if you eat ice cream?"

I have to admit, Fluidity is starting to sound better and better.

Layla's phone rings.

"Do you mind? It's Harm," she says.

Mind? Why would I mind? We just spent half an hour talking about you, and I didn't even get to explain what my fight with Rainie was about. What is there to mind?

I can't talk to Rainie about this, obviously, and May is not answering my texts. I briefly consider calling Match, but the idea of me trying to have a phone conversation with him about my friend troubles is comical.

Whatever.

I might as well just tell Rover. At least he never interrupts me.

26

After the incident at the pond, Rainie starts avoiding me, again, which means I spend most of the time by myself ... again. Yoga is my solace, the one time of the day where it doesn't feel so sad or lonely not to be speaking to anyone. Match is there for me in his own way. At lunch, he leaves Harm to the girls and comes to sit at my table. Not that we talk that much, but it's nice to have someone to sit with, anyway. He's caught on to the fact that it is not Harm I'm staring at.

"What happened between you and Rainie?" he asks one afternoon, as I'm staring in her direction.

"We ... had a fight," I say, deciding that I won't betray her secret, not even to Match.

"And?" he says.

"And what?"

"And what was the fight about?"

"She's mad that I want to go to source school in the fall." That is close enough to the truth.

"Uh huh. She's pretty attached to you." Attached to me? What?

"No. I don't think it's that. She just thinks identifying is stupid. She's totally swallowed all that individual self-expression stuff they feed us here."

"Is that what you think of this place?"

"I don't know. I just think there's nothing wrong with wanting to fit in somewhere. To belong. How did you end up here anyway? This is a long way from the Meadow."

He looks at me, as if he's deciding what version of the truth to tell me. It's the same thing I just did to him, so I guess I can't blame him.

"New Preston doesn't have a school for unidentifieds," he says, finally. "Most people who are unidentified just sign up for Earth school and try to pass, but my flaming finger kind of ruled that out. I couldn't go to Fire school either though, on account of I haven't developed an immunity to the flames. That left me ... pretty much nowhere. So, I dropped out. I haven't been to school in two years. I was a special case, I guess, so Fluidity offered to sponsor me. But I have to go to these sessions with a counselor each week. They're studying me. I'm like their little lab rat or something ... Whatever, it's cool. It beats hanging out in the Meadow all day and night."

Here goes.

"Um, Match," I say. "I know about the program. I was at the council meeting when you got up to talk."

"A'ight. So you know then."

"Yeah. I'm sorry about the council turning you down. Why didn't you tell me you were going to be there?"

"Didn't seem like you had much reason to know that. Why were you there?"

"Me? Oh. It's stupid. We're building this swimming pool in our yard." Suddenly, "stupid" seems like an understatement. "Never mind, it's not important. Is there anything I can do to help?"

"Not unless you have twenty thousand dollars lying around."

"I wish. I'm sorry."

"Don't sweat it. Liz says she's gonna put together another application for the city council in the fall. It just means my brother and sister will have to wait another semester at least before they can start high school. There's nowhere in the city that will take them."

Again, it seems important to say something meaningful, something to make myself worthy of his confidences.

"That sucks," I say. Double argh.

He smiles, and we eat the rest of our meal in silence.

27

Friday can't come fast enough. When it finally arrives, I text May as soon as I get home from camp. "U there?" Finally, she writes back.

"CJ, HI! Sorry cdnt write. No svc at GR. Cant wait to see u tmrw!!!"

God, I miss her! Suddenly, everything seems normal again. May is back (even if it is only for the weekend), and we're going to the Fourth of July fair together, just like we always do. I smile for the first time since my fight with Rainie.

Rainie. Thinking about our fight wipes the smile right back off my face.

Just then, Devon pokes his head in my door. He's wearing all black, and he is wielding a toilet plunger. When he sees me, he puts his finger to his lips and says, "Shhh." I smile and make the sign of zipping my lips. He pulls a calculator from his pocket, holds it to his ear and says, "Roger that, spy number one, over." Then, he tip-toes away.

A few minutes later, Matty knocks on the door, wearing only underwear and a Batman cape.

"Ceweste, hab you seem Debbin?" he asks.

"He went that way," I whisper, pointing in the direction Devon went.

What can I say? I'm a sucker for a three-year-old in underwear and a cape.

A minute later, I hear another knock on my door. I say "come in" without even looking up. My mom walks in, followed by Air—, I mean, Jackie. After what Rainie said, I have resolved to stop using that nickname, even in my head. The habit is a tough one to break.

"Celeste, can we talk?" asks my mom.

"Uh, sure," I say.

"Sweetie, you know we have rules about the Internet in this house."

"Yeah, so?"

She goes on, "So, we've discovered that you've been using the computer to access the Internet without permission."

"What do you mean, you 'discovered' this?" I ask.

Jackie responds, "A couple of months ago, your mom and I installed a program that tracks the Internet searches on our computer."

"What? You can't do that, that's a total invasion of privacy!"

My mom breaks in, "Celeste, we have always said that what happens on our family computer is our business, especially when it comes to the Internet. You kids are not old enough to—"

"So, what, am I, like, grounded? You wait until the night before May comes home to spring this on me!"

"No, Celeste, we are not going to ground you this time," says my mom. "We just want to talk to you about what we found."

Okay, breathe. I can still go to the fair tomorrow. But, wait. Oh my God, what did they see?

As if on cue, my mom answers my unspoken question, "We saw that someone had been running searches about 'faking' their source, and we knew that it couldn't be Layla, or anyone else—"

"Yeah, because I'm the only unidentified freak left in this house."

Jackie says, "Celeste, it's that kind of talk that's worrying us. We had no idea the pressure that you were feeling about this. We thought that maybe going to camp at Fluidity would help. Do you feel that it has?"

"I don't know."

My mom takes my hands in hers, "Celeste, it's important to us that you know that we don't expect you to be anything, anything, before you're ready. Source school can wait, okay, sweetie. It can wait."

"Fine. It can wait." I pull my hands back. "You don't have to worry about me, okay?" By now, tears are welling up in my mom's eyes. She must sense me closing off. Jackie lays her hand on my mom's arm and says to me, "Look, Celeste, I know that it may not be so easy for you to talk to us, or your dad, about this. That's why we made an appointment for you with Dr. Metzger."

"Who?"

My mom smiles at Jackie, takes control of her tears, and starts in, "Dr. Metzger is a source counselor. She's someone you can talk to about these things. Privately. She won't tell us, or anyone else. You can feel free to say whatever you want to her."

"Yeah," says Jackie. "Like, for instance, you can tell her that your Airhead stepmom has been annoying you and calling you CJ and you can't stand it. Stuff like that." She is smiling as she says this.

My face turns red. "I'm sorry about that," I say. "I guess I was having a bad day."

"It's okay," she says. "You're entitled to your feelings. Just remember, I have feelings too, okay? And I'm not the enemy. Your mom and I are here to help you, even if that means we need to give you space to work this out on your own. We just don't want you searching the Internet for help. It's not safe."

I look at my mom, "Do I really have to see a doctor? There's nothing wrong with me. I know that, okay?"

She says, "We'd like you to try one appointment. If you don't like it, or if it doesn't seem like a good fit, we'll talk."

I know better than to argue with my mom once she's signed me up for something. I decide this is not a battle I'm going to win. Besides, I'm worried that if I put up too much of a fight, they might change their minds about the fair. I can take one hour of this Dr. Metzger.

I think.

28

The next day, I put Rainie, Fluidity, and Dr. Metzger out of my mind, and I get ready for the fair. I pick out a red tee shirt with a sparkly, but subtle, American flag on the front, and I pair it with blue shorts and white sandals. To complete the look, I bedazzle my cheek with a few self-adhesive star-shaped "jewels." Perfect.

I'm standing at the front door when May arrives.

"CJ!" she screams, as she hops out of the back seat of her parents' minivan and runs over to me. "I missed you SO much! Oh my God, you look so good! Where did you get those stars?"

May is looking similarly festive. She also has a red shirt on, but instead of a flag, it has what looks like sequined fireworks on the front. She is wearing white cargo capris and flip flops. Her hair is drawn back in a ponytail, of course.

"Here, I saved you some," I say, pulling some more stars out of my pocket. Soon, we look like two members of a Fourth of July cheering squad. I yell back into the house, "Mom, May's here. I'm leaving!" Her reply drifts back from the kitchen, "Okay, sweetie. We'll be heading over later, so maybe we'll see you there. Have fun!"

Once we get to the fair, we arrange a place and time to meet back up with May's parents, and we set off to explore. The games section is a nightmare. There are little kid games, like the ring toss, or the one where you fish a rubber duckie out of a stream, and then there are source games, like fireball balloon pop or bobbing for apples.

I know, bobbing for apples sounds like something anyone can do, but have you ever bobbed for apples against a Water? I don't recommend it.

Anyway, I'm feeling pretty useless, so I suggest to May that we check out the rides. After nearly making ourselves sick on the gravitron, the tilt-a-whirl, and the tea cups, we hop on the ferris wheel, which gives us a chance to talk. May tells me all about Gray Rock, the counselors, the friends she's made. Then she lets it slip.

"I kissed a boy ... on the lips," she says, casually.

Seriously? Has anyone NOT kissed someone this summer? Just me, apparently.

"What? Oh my God!" I shriek, a little too loudly. The people in front of us look back to see what's going on. "You waited this long to tell me that? Who was it? What was it like?"

"His name is Noah," she says. "He is so cute! He lives in the city—"

"Forget the city," I say. "The kiss! What happened with the kiss?"

"I hardly remember the kiss at all. All I remember is that I was so nervous, the pee shot right down to my bladder, and I almost peed my pants!"

"Ewww," I say. "You are so gross!"

"I said 'almost.' I didn't actually do it! What about you? Have you met any cute boys at Fluidity?" I tell her about Match and Harm and how all the other girls at Fluidity fawn all over them.

"The 'other girls,' huh? But not you, right? What do you do then?"

Just then it seems wrong to keep anything from May. She's my best friend. I have to tell her everything. I just have to.

"I've kind of been hanging out with someone," I say.

"Yeah, who?"

"You know, Rainie."

"Very funny. I can just see it now. You and Rainie feeding the goats together."

She starts to laugh, but stops when she sees my face. "Oh my God, you're not kidding."

"Nope."

"You and Rainie?"

"Yup."

"What? Goats and everything?"

"Oh, yes, you would not believe the appetite on Raja—"

Now she's looking at me like I have two heads.

"Wow, I have been gone a long time," she says. "The way you talked about her, I just never thought you'd end up hanging out together."

"I know. Me neither. Except, the thing is, we're not actually speaking to each other right now." I tell her about the gloves and the fire and everything. She stares at me in disbelief.

Finally, she says, "What are you going to do? Are you going to tell your mom?"

"Why would I do that?"

We reach the bottom of the ferris wheel and get off. We start walking towards the meeting spot.

"You know, so she can get some help."

"Help for what?"

"For Rainie. It's not normal, CJ. She's a girl!"

"I know she's a girl. So what?"

"So, she needs to see a doctor. They can help her. They might be able to, you know, fix it."

"Okay, now I get why she's been trying to hide behind gloves all this time. Are you kidding me with this?" I can barely contain my anger.

"You're mad at *me*, now? You unload this insane story on me, and now you're upset when I try to help? What is the matter with you?"

"I just don't think you need to send someone to a doctor because they're a Fire. Why can't girls be Fire, anyway?"

"They just can't!"

May's parents walk up, and we both go silent. "Ready, girls?" asks May's mom with a smile. She is carrying an enormous eggplant with a blue first-place ribbon pinned to it.

"Congratulations, Mrs. Jacobs," I say, nodding toward the eggplant.

"Thank you, Celeste! Plenty more where that came from. Do you want to take this one home?"

"Uh, sure."

"All right, girls. Shall we?"

29

The ride back to my house is eerily quiet. The minute the car stops, I jump out, thank May's parents, and spit out a quick "bye" in May's direction. "Bye" is all she says. I stand and watch as the car drives away, a giant eggplant in my arms. It is dark outside, but the Langfords' lights are on, and I can hear music coming from the backyard.

I set down the eggplant on my front porch and head across the street towards the Langfords' house. I let myself in the gate to the side yard and walk around to the back. The music and singing is so loud that no one even notices my approach. There must be twenty or thirty people gathered around a fire pit. They cover every surface available, spilling out from the stone patio onto the lawn. They are lounging in lawn chairs, on blankets, or just sprawled out on the grass. Just about everyone has an instrument. I see guitars, violins, a banjo or two, a harp, and something else that I don't even recognize. Those who aren't playing are singing, or dancing ... or singing and dancing.

Rainie's mom spots me first. She is at the center of the sprawl, next to the fire.

"Celeste, so glad you could make it. Come! Sit!"

Suddenly, all eyes are on me, including Rainie's. She is sitting off to the side, eating a popsicle.

"I got this, Mom." she says.

Her mom shrugs, and the music resumes, full-tilt.

Rainie walks past me. I follow her to the front of the house where she sits down on the porch steps. She finishes her popsicle and sets the stick down on the steps next to her.

"Hey," I say, finally.

"Hey. I didn't think you were going to come tonight."

"Yeah, I wasn't, and then ... I changed my mind. Listen, can we talk about what happened on Monday?"

"What happened?"

"I don't know, your hands started smoking?"

"What about it?"

"Well, like, how long has that been happening?"

"I don't know, since last fall, I guess. You know, it was a lot easier in the winter. In the summer, it kind of sucks to have to wear these." She looks down at the leather gloves on her hands.

"You don't have to wear those," I say.

"Easy for you to say."

I sit down next to her and grab one of her forearms in my hand. With the other hand, I start to pull at fingertips of her glove. She pulls away at first, but then her arm relaxes. Finger by finger, I slide the glove off her hand. When I'm done, she extends her

125

other arm to me, and I ease the glove off. Underneath, her hands are white and wrinkled, like they've been soaking too long in water. It looks like some kind of surgical mistake, like someone attached the wrong pair of hands to her smooth, tanned arms.

"Rainie," I gasp. "You can't keep doing this to yourself. It's not healthy."

"It's a lot healthier than letting people know I'm a … a She-Fire. That's a good way to get your butt kicked."

"Oh yeah, well, let 'em try. You can fireball those worthless idiots."

She laughs. "Wow. I changed my mind. You're right. That sounds like a great way to make friends."

"Those aren't the kind of people you want as friends anyway." I tell her about my conversation with May and how angry it made me, that it has made me question how I was ever friends with May to begin with.

"Okay, so, what kind of friends do I want, exactly?" she asks. "The non-existent kind?"

"No. You want … my kind. Me. I'm your friend."

"Thanks, Swergie."

"Rainie?"

"Hmm?"

"Can you show me? I mean, can you do it without getting mad first?"

"Sure. I can do it whenever I want. It's just that I can't control it that well when I'm mad."

She gets up and turns off the porch light. She sits back down next to me, puts her right hand out, palm facing me, and lets the fire start to burn on her fingertips. The flames glow blue and purple in the dark. She picks up the popsicle stick from the steps next to her and lights it in the flames. The stick burns red and orange. The flames intermingle, creating a swirl of color. I'm mesmerized by it. Suddenly, she blows out the popsicle stick and gives her hand a shake, sending a final swarm of blue sparks circling towards the sky.

"Wow, Rainie, that's amazing. I mean, I've seen my brother do it, but he can't control it nearly the way you do."

"It takes some practice. Harm's been teaching me."

"He knows?"

"Yeah, I made him promise not to tell our parents."

"Why? They wouldn't care, would they?"

"No, they'd probably think it was amazing and want to take out an ad in the paper about it."

"Oh, right. What are you going to do? You can't wear gloves your whole life."

"I've been trying to learn to control it better. As soon as I can figure out—"

"What? How not to get mad? Have you seen how much annoying stuff there is in the world? I get mad five times on my way to school. No. You're gonna have to tell your parents."

"How do I do that?"

"Um, how about, 'Mom, Dad, I'm a Fire. Can you please pass the seaweed wraps?'"

She laughs. "Seaweed wraps? What exactly do you think goes on at my house?"

"Oh, don't go acting like you don't have seaweed wraps in there. I bet I could find ten different seaweed products in your kitchen. What do you want to bet?"

She's laughing really hard now. "Okay, I admit it. I'm a Fire, and I eat seaweed wraps. Call the news. Come see the freaky flamette and her seaweed products."

I say, still half-joking, "You know what the worst part of this is, for me?"

"For you? This ought to be good."

"The worst part is that now I really am the last person on earth to find out what my source is."

"I take it the garlic tea didn't do the trick."

"Nope. Nothing. Unless my goal was to discover the recipe for bad breath. Then it was very successful. … um, Rainie?"

"Yeah?"

"What are you going to do about school?"

"What do you mean?"

"I mean, are you going to go to DFS in the fall?"

"No way! Imagine me at DFS with all those Fire guys. Blech. Besides, how would that even work? I don't think they even have a girls' bathroom in there. No, I'm staying at Fluidity. I know my parents will let me. They didn't really want Harm to go to DFS in the first place, but he wanted to. I guess he likes all the Fire courses. He thought Fluidity was boring."

A car pulls into the Langfords' driveway, setting off the motion sensor light on the garage. It's the Langfords' Prius—with Harm and Layla inside. I'm bracing myself to witness another makeout session when Rainie shoots a fireball toward the car window. Harm looks up and sees us on the steps. Layla turns around and hops out of the car when she sees us. Just then, my mom opens the front door to our house across the street.

"Girls, are you out there? Come on inside. It's time to say good night." She spots the eggplant. "Oh, my lord, what is that thing?"

Layla whispers something in Harm's ear and runs across the street into the house. Harm disappears into the garage.

I turn to Rainie. "I'd better go. I'll see you Monday … without the gloves?"

"Without the gloves."

"Cool." I lean forward and hug her. Then I run across the street and into my house.

30

Back inside, things are pretty lively for 9:00 p.m. on a Saturday. The boys are usually asleep by now, but tonight, Devon is still awake. I can hear him in the kitchen, arguing with Jackie about why she won't let him take his new stuffed alligator to bed with him.

I start to climb the stairs, when I hear my mom and Layla on the second floor landing, arguing in a raised whisper.

My mom says, "I like Harm, too, sweetie. But I am not going to let you throw away everything you've worked for over a boy."

"I'm not throwing everything away. It's just for the summer. I thought you would like the idea. You've been talking about the place like it's God's gift to camps."

"It is a wonderful place. That's not the point."

"What is the point, then? Celeste gets to do whatever she wants, and I have to be a slave to you and Coach. You have no idea what it's like ..."

I decide that walking through the alligator fight would be the lesser of two evils, so I reverse course and head into the kitchen. With any luck, I can sneak up the back stairs and into my room without anyone noticing. Devon and Jackie are still going strong.

"Devon, you know the rules. Only special toys are allowed in bed because your hands can make fire at night. Give me the alligator, please."

"But, Mommy, I won't put it in my bed. I just want to look at it. I won't touch it. I promise." He clasps the toy close to his chest.

"I'm sorry, Devon. It's not okay. It's too dangerous."

"You never let me have anything in my room. Matty can sleep with whatever he wants. It's not fair!" With that, the flames start to flare up on his little fingertips.

"Devon!" The stuffed alligator has already caught fire. Jackie grabs it from him and puts out the flames in the sink. Devon yells, "You did that on purpose! You made me mad so my hands would flame. You are a mean Mommy!" Jackie has tears in her eyes. She stays facing the sink where Devon can't see her. Why did I think I could sneak through unnoticed? I walk up to Devon.

"Hi, D. I heard you got a new alligator."

"Yeah, I did. I won it at the fair. I was really good at shooting the balloons. They said I could have an alligator or a unicorn. But I didn't want a unicorn because that's for girls."

"Good choice."

"But now it's all wet and burned."

"Well, I have an idea. What if we put him in a special place to dry? We could make him a bed in the bathtub. Alligators like bathtubs."

"What kind of bed?"

"Um, like, a towel bed, so it's soft for him to sleep, and he can get dry, too."

"Okay."

Jackie hands me the soaking wet alligator and mouths the words "thank you." I smile at her and take Devon upstairs to get some towels. After we set up the alligator bed, I bring Devon into his room and read him a book. His eyes are half-closed when I finish. I plant a kiss on his forehead and head for the door.

"I love you, too," he murmurs, even though I haven't said anything.

"I love you," I whisper, to no one in particular, because Devon is already asleep.

I creep out of Devon's room as quietly as I can. I hear my mom and Jackie downstairs in the living room. Jackie is crying. I tip-toe down the stairs to listen. Jackie's voice says, "It's taking years off my life, Lena. I'm a nervous wreck. I don't know how other people survive this."

"Every Fire we know went through this as a boy, and they all came out okay. I know it's hard to watch, but the fire doesn't actually hurt him. And he'll learn to control it better. It just takes time."

"But he doesn't listen. I don't know any other way to explain it to him. Fire is dangerous. Who cares if it doesn't burn him? He could burn our house down. He just doesn't get it."

"He will."

"What was Layla so upset about?"

"It's ridiculous, really. One date with Harm, and she's ready to quit swimming and go to Fluidity with him for the summer."

"What did you tell her?"

"I told her I wasn't about to let her give up her life's dream for a boy, even a very nice boy."

"Would it have to mean giving up swimming altogether? Couldn't she go to morning practices and spend the rest of the day at Fluidity?"

"Jackie, I didn't tell you this so that you could encourage her. This is the last thing she needs."

"Why are you immediately closed off to the idea? It's the summer. Let her have some fun. She works too hard. She's only sixteen."

"Only sixteen? The Olympics are in three years. She could be on that team. But not if she throws it all away for a boy. She's been working for this since she was eight years old. I don't expect you to understand."

"Right. I get it. I've only been around for a couple of years, so I'm not qualified to have an opinion. Well, I'm here now, and I see what she goes through week after week. She's going to burn out, Lena."

"Please don't sit there and try to tell me what's best for my own daughter—"

"*Your* daughter. Right. She's only *our* daughter until we disagree about something. Is that it?"

Things are starting to get ugly. As curious as I am about what's happening with Layla, I can't stand to sit through one more fight this evening. I walk the rest of the way down the stairs, making sure they can hear my footsteps.

My mom and Jackie put the brakes on their fight, and my mom walks over to meet me at the bottom of the stairs. "Celeste, honey, thank you for putting Devon to bed." She leans in and kisses me on the top of the head. "Now it's your turn to get tucked in."

31

On Sunday, the tension still has not left the house. Layla is not talking to my mom, and my mom and Jackie are only speaking to each other in short, businesslike sentences. Harm comes over in the morning and asks to take Layla to her meet. For once, my mom doesn't protest. After a lunch so quiet you could hear a pin drop, Jackie takes the boys to the park to run around. This leaves me alone at home with my mom. This never happens. As much as I hate all the tension, it's almost worth it to get to spend some time alone with her.

Our project for the afternoon is to figure out what to do with Mrs. Jacobs's mutant eggplant. We search the Web for recipes and end up making a monster batch of eggplant parmesan for dinner. The mood at dinner is still a bit tense, but the food is good, if I do say so myself.

That night, I dream that I'm in a garden. Enormous eggplants hang all around me. I reach for one, but as my hand draws closer, the vines pull away, keeping it out of reach. Come. Here. I need you. Why won't you bend to me? What is the matter with you? What is the matter with me? ... I wake up in a puddle of sweat, ready to kick some vegetable butt.

32

It's Monday morning. I get out of bed and open my door just in time to see Matty waddle by with a pull-up diaper around his ankles and a spatula in his hand.

"Mowning, Ceweste."

"Morning."

Sometimes it's better not to ask.

I'm too excited to eat breakfast, so I grab a bar from the pantry and tell my mom that I'm getting a ride with the Langfords. I run across the street and ring the bell. Rainie opens the door. Flowered sundress, leather boots, but no gloves. Her hands are still much lighter than the rest of her body, but the wrinkles have gone away. Well, it's a start.

Rainie smiles. "Come on in, we're almost ready."

She grabs my arm and pulls me inside. A shiver goes through my body. I realize that this is the first time she's touched me—I mean, really touched me—without the gloves. Her hands are smooth … and soft. I guess wearing gloves every day for nine months helps keep the moisture in.

We get to camp, and by noon, Rainie is a celebrity. Everyone we see wants her to flare up. It gets old pretty quickly. I mean, imagine you're on your yoga mat in relaxation pose and someone just marches up and asks you to set fire to your fingers. Annoying.

Even the adults are acting weird around her, asking her how she's handling it, and if she wants to talk. She does not. Later that afternoon, we finally ditch everyone and go to the meeting house to hide. A few people are sitting inside, meditating.

We slip in the back and try to keep a low profile. Except for morning meeting, I've never really spent much time in here. Rainie sits cross-legged, with her hands palms-up on her knees. She closes her eyes and lets out a deep breath. Okaaay.

I do my best imitation of what I've just seen her do, then sit there for about thirty seconds before I open my eyes to see what's going on. Rainie is still sitting quietly, with her eyes closed. "Now what?" I whisper to her. She opens one eye. "Just ... be," she says, and shuts her eye again.

Oh, brother.

Not knowing what else to do, I close my eyes and just sit. A breeze drifts through the open windows of the meeting house. Someone has lit some vanilla incense in the front of the room. The smell creeps closer to me, mixed with the scent of cut grass from the lawn outside, and the faint, but distinct, odor of the goat barn. I can hear the clanging of the wind chimes that hang on the porch outside, the sound of voices down by the pond, and the now familiar bleating of Raja, Pippa, Orzo, and Melanie.

The breeze ebbs and flows. It gusts just enough to lift the hair from my neck, then subsides. When the breeze lets up, I can feel the heat of the afternoon sun, angling in through the window onto my right arm and knee.

My mind wanders, and I begin to retrace the events of the past weekend. Recalling the fight with May makes my chest tighten. What is her problem? Why does she care if Rainie is a Fire? Never in my life have I thought of May as prejudiced or closed-minded. Has she been this way the whole time, and I never realized it? No, that can't be.

I met May on my first day of school in Darwin. After the divorce. After we moved. After my summer with Rainie. The desks in the classroom were arranged in clusters of four, two on each side, facing each other. May had the desk next to mine. Across from us were two boys whose whole purpose in life was to annoy us. I guess we bonded over how much we couldn't stand them.

May had a lot of friends. She didn't need me. But, for some reason, we just clicked, and soon we were inseparable. She wanted to join the soccer team, so I joined the soccer team. She wanted to learn to play the flute, so I learned to play the flute.

And we were popular. People would ask to eat lunch with us, and we'd say, "maybe next Tuesday, our table is full this week." We were invited to all the birthday parties, and any club we joined was instantly flooded with members. We ruled. I loved my new life, and I owed it all to May.

Then Jackie came along. When my mom started dating her, I thought my world was going to unravel. How could she *do* that to me? At first, it didn't affect me much. My mom would go out with Jackie when Layla and I were at our dad's house. I hardly ever saw her. But after a while, Jackie started coming to my soccer games and recitals and stuff. How was I supposed to explain that? For a while, I told people she was my aunt from out of town … or a cousin from out of town … or a friend from out of town. The problem was, she never left town. And she and my mom just got more and more serious.

When I found out Jackie and the boys were going to move in with us, I knew I couldn't keep it hidden any longer. So, I told May. She just smiled at me and said, "CJ, no one ever thought she was your aunt. What's the big deal? It does suck to live with boys, though. My brother is a pig."

And that was it. May could make anything okay. She would talk about my mom and stepmom at school, like it was no big deal, and everyone else followed her lead. She was that magnetic. So, what happened to her? Why is this thing with Rainie any different?

Questions like this are still running through my mind when Rainie grabs my arm and shakes it.

"Swergie! Snap out of it. It's time to go home."

"Home? You mean we've been sitting here for, like, an hour?"

I guess I know how to meditate better than I thought.

33

Dr. Metzger's office is out of another century. Lava lamps. Shag carpet. It looks like she decorated the place with stuff from my mom's attic. I'm sitting on a purple velvet couch, wishing I was someplace else.

Dr. Metzger is sitting in a chair opposite me. She has on a long, flowing skirt, a peasant blouse, and a necklace of ridiculously-large wooden beads. She doesn't look like any doctor I've ever seen.

"So, Celeste, I think your moms told you I am a source counselor."

"My mom. I only have one."

"Of course. Your mom and … how do you like to refer to her?"

"Jackie."

"Of course, Jackie."

"Now, I think your mom and Jackie told you that I am a source counselor. And that is true. But I want you to know that I am here to talk to you about anything, not just your source. Feelings, hopes, fears. Anything. Okay?"

"Uh, okay."

"Is there anything you would like to talk about?"

"Um, not really."

"Oh, well this should be a short meeting then." She laughs a little too hard at her own joke. "No, seriously, if you don't have something you want to start with, I have some questions I would like to ask. Of course, you only need to answer if you feel comfortable doing so."

"Okay."

"What did you think when your moms asked you to meet with me?"

"My mom and Jackie, you mean? They didn't *ask* me, exactly. More like, told me."

"Oh, I see. They told you. How did it make you feel to be told?"

"Make me feel? Um, okay, I guess."

"Did part of you want to come here?"

"Part of me? Like my arms or legs?"

"No. I guess I'm asking whether you see this session as an opportunity or an obligation."

"I don't really 'see' it as anything. I'm just here."

It's getting harder and harder for Dr. Metzger to mask her frustration with my responses, and harder and harder for me not to laugh. What is the purpose of this, I wonder? Do people really get something out of this?

At the end of the hour, Dr. Metzger and I have our first bonding moment when we see that time is up and simultaneously breathe a sigh of relief. She quickly recovers, however, and says in an optimistic tone, "Okay, Celeste, it was wonderful to meet you.

I'm going to take a moment to meet with your mom. I look forward to our next session."

Dream on, lady. There will be no next session.

* * *

"What do you mean, I have to go back?" I scream at my mom in the car.

"Dr. Metzger said that one session is really not enough. And I agree. I understand why you didn't want to open up right away. You just met her. It's natural."

"Who says I didn't want to open up? She talked to you about what I said? I thought she wasn't supposed to do that!"

"No, no. She didn't tell me what you talked about. Just that you seemed … reluctant to open up."

"Well, I am reluctant. Counseling is stupid. I'd rather be at camp."

"I'm glad to hear you are enjoying camp more. I know Rainie's mom says she's been happier than ever since you got there. And imagine, all that time, Rainie, a Fire. Incredible." Happier than ever? With me?

"Still," my mom adds, "the fall is coming, and we have school to think about. Dr. Metzger can help you come to some resolution about that."

"I thought you said source school could wait, and I didn't need to worry about that?"

"I still think that, sweetie. I'd be perfectly happy to send you to Fluidity next year. But, is that what you want?" She turns her head to me briefly, then turns back to the road. She doesn't press me for an answer. I wish I had one to give her.

34

That night after dinner, my mom invites me to join her at a fundraising meeting for the Fluidity pilot program that she is co-hosting with Rainie's mom over at the Langfords' house. Why not? It'll beat trying to make conversation with Jackie while my mom is out, and anyway, seeing Rainie will be fun.

We are the first to arrive. Rainie's mom invites us in, and my mom volunteers my help in setting out the snacks. Rainie is in the kitchen pouring salsa into a bowl.

"Hi, Ms. Jardine. Hey, Celeste," she says. "Mom, how many bowls of salsa do we need?"

"One should be enough, honey. I think it's only going to be six of us tonight."

"Only six?" asks my mom. "What happened to Margaret and all the other PTA moms?"

"Margaret's coming. But only one other person RSVP'ed. With you, me, Liz, and Louise Robbins, that's six."

"I can't believe it. They all acted so interested when I brought it up the other night."

"Well, lots of people are out of town on vacation. This just isn't a great time for people, apparently."

"Oh well, at least we can lay the groundwork. We may have to postpone our efforts to the fall when everyone's schedules settle down a bit."

"The fall," I say, "but that's too late. Match's brother and sister ... they should be in school by then."

"I know, sweetie, but if we do anything now, we'll raise just a fraction of what we can make during the school year. We need to concentrate our efforts on making the most money for the program."

I frown and grab a bowl of some weird-looking black strips off the counter. Is this food?

"Is this supposed to go to the living room?" I ask.

"Oh, yes, the nori. That should go on the coffee table with the other snacks."

"Nori?" I ask.

"They're seaweed crisps. Packed with vitamins."

"Seaweed. You don't say." I look over at Rainie and mouth the words, "I KNEW IT!"

We both burst out laughing.

"Something funny, girls?" my mom asks.

"Nothing," I say. "Just a little seaweed humor."

We scurry off to put the snacks on the coffee table, then retreat to Rainie's bedroom on the second floor. Rainie opens a window and puts on some music.

"Mind if I light some incense?" she asks.

I shake my head.

She props up a stick of incense in a small bowl of dry rice and lights it with her finger. We lay back on her bed, looking up at the ceiling. She has a piece of fabric tacked up precariously over her bed. The way it billows out toward the floor makes it look like a sail full of wind. I recognize the symbol in the middle as an "om."

"You're really into that stuff, huh?" I ask.

"That stuff?"

"The meditation and incense and stuff."

"Yeah. Why not? What's the matter—you don't like it?"

"No, I'm just not used to it. It seems so weird to sit and do nothing."

"It's not nothing. It's actually a skill. To be able to separate yourself from your thoughts and just, sort of, watch them wander by. Plus, when I have my eyes closed like that, I can feel my other senses get so much sharper. Here, sit up."

I sit up and we turn towards each other, sitting cross-legged.

"Put your hands palms up on your knees. Now close your eyes and let go of your thoughts. Whatever happens, don't open your eyes."

Whatever happens?

I sit in anticipation. My skin is already tingling and nothing has even happened yet. Then, without a word, she picks up one of my hands and cradles it in her palm. A breeze shoots through the room, and all the hairs stand up on the back of my neck. With her free hand, Rainie starts to make small circles in my palm with her fingertips. Her fingers move to the sensitive part of my wrist, just beyond the heel of my palm. Then she ventures further, her fingers traveling lightly up and down the inside of my forearm. The effect is electric ... and terrifying.

Flustered, I open my eyes and pull my arm away.

"Yeah, um, I see what you mean."

She smiles at me.

"Want me to do the other arm? I don't want you to be unbalanced."

"No, thanks. That's okay. I think we should go back downstairs. I don't want to miss the whole meeting. I need to ask Liz something."

She frowns. "Oh. Okay."

When we get to the living room, the mood is pretty tense. Rainie's mom has the floor.

"Liz, my point is, is this the paradigm we want to be perpetuating? This idea that everyone has to identify. I mean, since when does being unidentified have to be a disorder. As you know, I am unidentified and proud, and so is my husband. I thought that Fluidity was a place where unidentified teens could find acceptance. By promoting this pro-identification program, aren't you sending them mixed messages?"

Liz responds, "I hear what you are saying, Debbie. And I agree with you that not everyone can be put in the same box. It could well be that some people don't naturally gravitate toward a single source. But you need to see these statistics. There is something else going on here. Something about the environment that these kids are growing up in is inhibiting their natural development, whatever that might be. And it is affecting them negatively. Look at Tyrone."

Just then, I spot Match's grandmother, sitting over next to my mom.

"My grandchildren need this, Miss Langford. Things can't go on this way. They need an education. It's that simple. If there was a school for them in the city that would be one thing ..."

"I hear you, Louise, and I agree, of course. I just want to be careful about the message we are sending."

My mom breaks in, "Okay, it sounds like before we can get to the real planning, we are going to have to work on developing a mission statement that we can all agree upon."

Mission statement? How long is that gonna take?

My mom continues, "Let me see if I can work on something for our next meeting in September. By then, we should have quite a few more volunteers."

September? For a mission statement? Are these people insane?

Match's grandmother looks just as frustrated as I am. Still, she is diplomatic.

"Thank you so much for your help, Miss Jardine." And to the group, she says, "I can't tell you how much this all means to me and my family." As she looks around the room, she spots me and Rainie.

"Well, hello there, girls. You must be Rainie and Celeste. Tyrone has talked a lot about you and the young man, what's his name?

"Harmony," says Rainie's mom.

"Oh, yes," she says. "Well, I sure hope that we will be seeing you at Match's birthday party a week from Saturday. He sure would love that."

Birthday party? What? I look next to me, and Rainie is looking just as surprised.

"Of course," says my mom, "Let me get your address. Celeste's dad lives in New Preston. I'm sure he won't mind getting them there."

Yeah, but does she realize we've been banned from ever setting foot in that neighborhood? Never mind that. First things first. This coming Saturday I'm staying at my dad's alone because Layla is sleeping over at a friend's house. My dad said I could have Rainie over for the night. The thought of it sends tingles up my spine. What is happening to me?

35

Saturday night finally arrives. I'm at my dad's apartment, waiting for Rainie. Harm is going to drop her off, then go downtown to meet up with Match. The buzzer rings, and I tell the doorman to send Rainie up. I wait in the doorway to the apartment, until she steps off the elevator.

"Oh my God, Celeste. This place is sick! Why didn't you tell me your dad was rich?"

"He's not that rich," I say. He is that rich.

Rainie is in her full-on badass gear: vintage sundress over ripped skinny jeans, boots, and copious amounts of dark eyeliner. I wouldn't approach her in a dark alley.

"Come on," she says. "Harm's waiting."

"Waiting? I thought he was just dropping you off."

"That was before Match got us all tickets to a concert downtown. I'm sure your dad won't mind if we're with my brother."

Rainie works her spell on my dad, and before I know it, we're heading downtown in the Langfords' Prius, with Rainie applying makeup to my face between stoplights. She even brought clothes for me to change into.

By the time we meet up with Match, I'm looking about five years older, and a whole lot tougher. Well, as tough as it's possible to look when you're a blonde-haired, blue-eyed girl from Darwin. Okay, let's face it, I look a little bit like Alterna-Rock Barbie.

The "concert," as it turns out, is a band playing at a dive bar in downtown New Preston. A line of people snakes down the sidewalk outside the front door. Match is waiting for us near the front. The guy at the door asks us for ID. Match is the only one who has any, and he starts arguing with the bouncer to let us in. After about ten minutes of this, we cut our losses and decide it would be just as much fun to play pool in the under twenty-one club across town. Harm and Match drop us at the door with instructions to reserve a table, while they go to park the car. We're winding our way through the tables with a tray of billiard balls when I see her.

May is standing at a table near the back of the club, pool cue in hand, with a bunch of people I don't recognize. Gray Rock kids, I'm sure. Let's just say they look about as different from me and Rainie as is humanly possible. The guys are in pressed jeans, Polo shirts, and baseball caps, and the girls are wearing dresses, cardigan sweaters, and strappy sandals. May included. She is smiling and flirtatious, casually putting her arms around one of the guys. Noah, no doubt.

Rainie stakes out the table next to them, and I'm just about to call her off, when May spots me.

"CJ?" she says, clearly caught off guard.

Rainie looks at me, quizzically.

"Hello, May," I say.

Now Rainie's face floods with recognition, and I see her cheeks flush. Uh oh … down, girl. Maybe I shouldn't have told her what May said about her needing medical help.

"Who's your friend?" asks the guy next to May, putting his arm around her.

"Noah, this is CJ," says May, "and …"

"Rainie," I fill in. "Rainie, this is May … and Noah."

Rainie extends her hand to Noah. Noah leans into May and whispers, "Is she the … you know?"

"The what?" demands Rainie, her face getting hotter.

"Noah, let's just go play, okay?" May pleads, tugging at his arm.

By now we have caught the attention of the rest of the Gray Rock group. Noah announces, "Look, it's May's friend, CJ, and her pal, Rainie. You know, the one she told us about." I shoot a look at May, who looks back at me with apologetic eyes. My eyes tell her that I don't accept her apology.

"Rainie, don't give them the satisfaction," I say. But she is too hot. Any minute, she's going to flare up. Just then, Harm and Match arrive, carrying drinks. Harm sizes up the situation and immediately hands Rainie a cold glass of soda. By now, as usual, all eyes are on Match. Although, to his credit, Harm is getting his share of appraising looks from the Gray Rock girls. That's right. Eat your hearts out, ladies. They're with us.

Match keeps his eyes on Noah and says, "Everything okay, Celeste?"

"Everything's fine," I say, and for good measure, I pull Match down by his shirt and give him a big kiss on the lips. Beat that, May.

Everyone freezes.

Only Match keeps his composure. "Well, I'm sorry your friends couldn't stay longer," he says, putting his arm around me. The Gray Rock crew takes the hint and leaves. On the way out, May grabs my arm and whispers, "CJ, I really am sorry."

"So am I," I say.

After May and her friends clear out, Match and I turn around to see Harm and Rainie with their mouths wide open, staring at us.

"Relax," he says. "We were just messing with them. Right, Celeste?"

"Yeah, of course," I say. Rainie looks relieved. Or am I imagining it? This night has been so bizarre. It's hard to tell what's real and what's not.

After that, things settle down, and we manage to have some fun playing pool, betting each other the right to unload unpopular chores at camp. After a humiliating loss to Harm, which earns me the pleasure of feeding the goats whenever that chore is assigned to him over the next two weeks, I excuse myself to go to the bathroom.

Match comes up behind me as I'm about to go into the ladies' room.

"Hey, C, are you okay?"

"Yeah, it's fine. I've fed the goats before."

"Not that. I mean, about the kiss. That was a joke, right?"

Yeah. But you don't have to be so happy about that fact.

"Yeah, of course."

"Okay, I just wanted to make sure. You know you're like a little sister to me, right?" He punches me on the arm.

"Right, *brother*." I punch him back.

"Good. So cut it out. I'm way older than you. You could get me in trouble pulling stuff like that."

"I know. Seventeen next week, right?"

He looks surprised. Wow. Match, off his guard? There's a first for everything.

I say, "Your grandma invited us to your party. We were gonna surprise you. Oops."

"You're coming to my place?"

"That's where the party is, right?"

"Yeah, it's just ..."

"Don't worry about us, okay? We're gonna come whether you like it or not, so deal with it."

"A'ight. Don't say I didn't warn you."

"Relax," I say, "It'll be fine. Can I pee now?"

He holds his hands up and backs away. "Don't let me stop you."

Okay. Well, I guess if I had any confusion about how Match feels about me, that "sister" comment pretty much cleared it up. But how do I feel about him?

36

Later, in my room at my dad's apartment, I'm lying in my bed awake, with Pumpkin curled up on my stomach. I look down at Rainie, who's asleep on the pull-out trundle bed, just below me. All the make-up is off, and she looks younger, more innocent. Also, I realize this is the first time in a while that I've seen her without a scowl on her face. It's like she's been trying to build a hard exterior to keep the fire within her at bay. A human bomb shelter.

In this light, she looks soft, almost fragile. I recall the softness of her hands on my arm, and a shudder goes through me.

Why didn't I feel that same shudder when I kissed Match tonight? Was it the fact that everyone was looking at us? Or that I knew it was just for show? Whatever it was, I was nowhere close to peeing my pants.

I push Pumpkin off me and roll over to the edge of the bed. On a whim, I reach down and run my fingers along Rainie's bare arm. Like clockwork, my skin starts to tingle, and a shudder goes through my entire body. She shifts in her sleep, and I panic, rolling back over toward the wall.

I force my mind away from Rainie and think about May instead. What has happened to her? It's like she's letting Noah and that Gray Rock crew walk all over her. That's not the May I know. The May I know would have stood up for Rainie and told Noah to knock it off if he knew what was good for him. What is she so afraid of?

The questions keep coming until fatigue takes over, and I finally succumb to sleep.

37

The following week, I'm in my session with Dr. Metzger, and I'm about to explode. I'm ensconced in the purple couch, staring at the clock, mentally counting the ways in which I'm annoyed. One, I'm annoyed with my mom for making me come here. Two, I'm annoyed with Dr. Metzger for sitting there quietly, just staring at me. Three, I'm annoyed with the universe for existing. There, that should cover it.

Suddenly, Dr. Metzger says, "It's okay to be mad at me, Celeste. I can take it."

"Why would I be mad at you? I don't even know you."

"Sometimes, we get so angry, it just sprays out in every direction. This is a safe place to let that happen."

"What makes you think you know anything about me?"

"I only know what you choose to tell me, and so far, I admit, that's not much. But I also know what I see, and right now I see a very angry, very scared young woman in front of me."

"Scared? I am NOT scared. Pissed off, yes. Annoyed, yes. Scared, no."

"The idea that you might not be admitted to source school next fall ... that doesn't scare you?"

"I can't ... I can't even think about next fall. I can't even make it through a single week without something in my life falling apart."

The tears are coming now, but I keep talking. Talking about Rainie being a Fire, about my fight with May, about the confrontation in the club, everything. Every once in a while I pause, and Dr. Metzger asks a question. Then I'm off and running again, with no end in sight. The hour passes in a heartbeat.

When it's time for me to leave, Dr. Metzger says, "Celeste, I hear that you're feeling overwhelmed by many things that are happening right now. This is an intense time. But if there is one thing you should keep in mind, it is that you are not alone in this. I'm here to support you, and so is your family. Just the fact that your parents brought you here means that they are committed to giving you all the tools you need to navigate this time in your life. Don't forget that."

The ride home is quiet. I feel empty, but almost in a good way. Like the weight of everything that has been happening has just been lifted a little.

Dinner that night is tense as usual, but it doesn't bother me so much. I just sit quietly and observe. Jackie is going on about how long it will take the concrete to set around the pool, Layla is giving my mom the silent treatment, and Devon and Matty are taking turns trying to slip peas into each other's glasses of milk. Devon is up by four.

I'm tuning in and out, when I hear Jackie say, ". . . should be ready for your birthday. . . Celeste?"

"I'm sorry. What?"

"I said, the builder said the pool should be ready for your birthday. What about a pool party?"

"Oh, yeah. That sounds great." My birthday. All this drama with May and Rainie, and I haven't even thought about the fact that my birthday is only three weeks away.

There's that weight again.

After dinner, I wander outside and find myself in front of the Langfords' house. Rainie sees me out the window and comes outside.

"Hey," she says. "Why didn't you ring the bell?"

"I don't know. It's kind of late."

"It's 7:30."

"Right. I guess I wasn't sure if I felt like talking. You know my birthday's coming up."

"Yeah, I know. I'm kind of hoping I'll be invited to the party this year," she jokes.

"I know you think this is stupid, but I told myself that by the time I turned fourteen, I would find out what my source was."

Rainie frowns. "Celeste, how can you put a deadline on something that you have no control over? Besides, maybe you're better off not knowing. Don't try to tell me that my life has gotten any easier since I figured out I'm a Fire. Can't you just try to relax and forget about it? What's the worst thing that could happen? You end up at Fluidity with me." She smiles.

"I know you're right," I say. "And, yes, you're invited to my birthday party!"

I give her a hug and head back across the street. I wish that what she said had made it all better, but the truth is, I'm still not sure I want to end up at Fluidity. A part of me still wants to be at DES next year, ruling the school with May.

May, who I haven't spoken to since our run-in in the city.

Who am I kidding? That life is over. I might as well try to accept it.

38

"Are you insane?" I hear my dad say through the phone. My mom has just given him Match's address for the birthday party on Saturday. "Lena, what were you thinking, telling her she could go there? She'll need an armed escort."

"Well, I couldn't just say no. It's one of Celeste's best friends from camp. His grandmother was right there asking me. What should I have said? 'I'm sorry, I wouldn't let my daughter set foot in the neighborhood where you and your grandchildren have lived your whole lives?' I trust you, Dennis. Just ... figure something out. I'd do it myself, but someone has to take Layla to her meet, and it makes more sense for me to do that ... yes, fine ... okay, good bye."

"Well?" I ask.

"Well, you're going to Match's party."

"I am?"

"Yes. Your father's in charge of getting you there. You should ask Rainie and Harm if they need a ride."

"Thank you, thank you, thank you! You are the best!"

I give my mom a big hug and kiss and run across the street to tell Rainie. This weekend, we're going to the Meadow!

* * *

Saturday morning finally arrives, and Harm, Rainie, and I hop into the Prius and head for my dad's. Apparently, the only way my dad felt comfortable with this idea was if he came with us to the party. Harm parks in one of my dad's spots in the garage, and we take the elevator up to the apartment. I use my key to get in.

"Dad, we're here!" I yell. "Are you ready?"

He ducks his head into the front hall. His left hand is holding a cell phone to his ear. He uses his right to quiet me, by putting his index finger to his lips.

"All right. No. I'll have my phone with me if you need to reach me. Thanks, Marshall." He hangs up, and turns to greet us. "Hello, kids. All here? Okay. I'll call down for a car."

"We don't need a car, Dad. Harm can drive."

"I don't think that's a good idea, sweetie." To Harm, "It's not that I don't trust you, Harm. It's just … not a good idea to park there."

Harm nods.

I say, "Oh. We're not taking a limo, are we?"

"Why do you ask?"

"I just don't want to look like an idiot, pulling up in a car like that."

"I understand. Don't worry, we're taking a town car."

"Okay, I guess."

"Well, you don't really have a choice in this one, I'm afraid."

He calls the car service, and we troop back down to the front lobby.

The doorman tips his cap at us, "Mr. Jardine, young Miss Jardine, lovely to see you today."

"Hi, Jake," I say.

Rainie gives Jake an awkward wave. "Hi," she says.

"Hey, man," says Harm.

Harm, Rainie, and I pile into the back seat of the town car, and my dad climbs into the front passenger seat. He gives the driver the address, and we're off. My dad's apartment is on a wide, divided avenue, with trees lining the median and the sidewalks on either side of the street. It is a neighborhood of luxury high-rise apartment buildings, with delis, coffee shops, and dry cleaners populating most of the commercial space on the ground level. As we travel south, the residential buildings start to give way to office complexes and large department stores. Then, we hit the theater district, with its neon lights and billboards. There are restaurants, bars, movie theaters, you name it. More residential after that, but on a smaller scale. Town houses. Small apartment buildings. A few shops. Fewer trees. This part of the city seems to go on for ages. Block after block goes by. Now each block we pass has one or two buildings boarded up. The storefronts all have metal gates. The streets haven't been cleaned in a while. If ever.

Ahead of us, I see three enormous high-rises sticking out above the townhouses. This is the

Meadow that I've seen on TV. We pull up in front of the metal gate that leads to the courtyard. We get out, and my dad says to the driver, "Thank you. I'll give you a call when we're ready to be picked up. It'll be before five."

We follow my dad over to the first of the three high-rises. No buzzer. No doorman. We walk right in and over to the elevators. The place is deserted. Up on the eighth floor, the only people we see are two young girls playing in the hallway. When they see us, they stop playing and duck inside an apartment down at the end of the hall.

"Eight twenty-six. This is it." says my dad. I can hear the sounds of music and laughter on the other side of the door. He knocks, and the music turns down inside.

"Well, see who it is," yells a woman's voice.

"There's some white dude at your door," says another, closer voice.

"Outta my way," yells the woman. "Who raised you?"

The door opens, and Match's grandmother greets us with a smile.

Someone turns the music back up, and she pulls us inside. The front door leads directly into the apartment's main living area. It's small, or it just appears that way because it is packed with people. To the left, through the throng, I can make out a small L-shaped kitchen that is separated from the living area by a pink formica countertop. Beyond the kitchen is a hallway that I assume leads to the bedrooms.

The aroma of barbecue sauce fills the room. My mouth starts to water.

"Mr. Jardine, welcome! Miss Jardine told me you'd be comin' with these three." She tilts her head back toward the living area. "Tyrone, baby, come on over here and say 'hello' to your friends! Mr. Jardine, you come with me. Let's get you something to eat."

Match's grandmother leads my dad through the crowd toward the kitchen. Rainie, Harm, and I stand trapped by the door. I start to have a strange realization. We are the only white people in the room. I might as well be neon green because I feel like a complete alien. I can't believe I used to feel out of place at my middle school in Darwin. That was nothing compared to this. Another realization. This is what Match must feel like every day at Fluidity.

After the longest minute and a half of my life, Match comes through the crowd to greet us. He and Harm clasp hands like they're about to arm wrestle, and Match gives Harm a slap on the back with his free hand. Then he reaches out his hands toward me and Rainie and musses up our hair as if we're little kids.

"You guys came. I can't believe it," he says.

"Of course, man," says Harm. "Like we'd miss your seventeenth!"

"Wait here. I want you to meet someone. Jazz, Ches, get over here!"

I recognize Match's brother and sister from the council meeting. They dart over at Match's command.

"Harm, Rainie, Celeste, this is my baby brother, Michael, and my sister, Jasmine."

"Hi," says Jazz. "He talks about you all the time. It's like we know you already."

"Yeah, we heard about you a'ight," Michael says, looking directly at Rainie. "Call me Ches." The hairs on the back of my neck start to stand up. What is that about?

"How do you get Ches from Michael?" Rainie asks.

"Once Match got his name, I thought it was so cool, I kept following him around sayin' if he's Match, then I'm Mat*ches*." He makes a peace sign with his right hand and the first two fingers light up. "Only the last part stuck."

"Impressive. What does that make me then?" She holds up both hands and blue flames engulf them. Is she flirting with him?

"Damn, girl. That's sick. You gotta show my cousins that."

With that, he drags her off into the crowd. She looks back at me and winks, as he tugs her out of sight.

"I better keep an eye on that," says Harm.

"No lie," says Match. And they follow Ches and Rainie into the crowd.

That leaves me alone with Jasmine.

"I guess I don't have to ask you where Jazz comes from," I say, lamely.

"Yeah, that one's pretty obvious," says Jazz. "You have a nickname?"

"Um, I seem to have one for every day of the week. Some people call me CJ. Rainie calls me Swergie. And your brother seems to like to call me C. Take your pick."

"A'ight, CJ, then."

I guess I told her to take her pick, but her saying CJ sounds wrong. Immediately, it makes me think of May. We've had no contact at all since the pool hall.

Could that be the last time I'll ever talk to her? The idea makes me nauseous.

"You okay?" asks Jazz.

"Yeah, I'm just, a little thirsty. Do you have anything to drink?"

"Sure," she says. "Follow me."

We make our way to the kitchen, and I pour myself a cup of Coke to help settle my stomach. The sugar and caffeine perk me right up. My mom never lets me have this stuff.

"Something smells really good," I say.

"That's my grandma's chicken wings," says Jazz. "You have to try some."

"Don't mind if I do," I say.

She laughs. Did I just say something funny?

"Help yourself," she says. "I'm gonna go see what Ches is up to. Bring your food and come find us."

"Okay."

She heads for the corner of the living room, where I see periodic blue flashes, accompanied by cheers and roars of laughter.

I fill up a plate from the food laid out on the kitchen counter. Barbecued chicken wings, mashed potatoes, salad. Yum. Just beyond the countertop, in the living room is a small round table and chairs. My dad is eating a plate of chicken wings, while Match's grandmother shows him a photo album. Baby pictures of Match? What I wouldn't give to see that. But I decide I'm more interested in seeing what Rainie is up to in the corner with Ches and the others.

I reach Rainie, and she gives me a big hug, almost knocking over my plate of food.

"Swergie, finally," she says. "Where have you been?"

I nod toward the food.

"Oh my God, that smells so good," she says. "I have to go get some of that."

"You can share mine," I say. "I took way too much."

Ches breaks into our little twosome.

"Rainie, one more time!"

"Okay," she says, "but this is the last one. I'm hungry!"

Ches turns around, and she stands behind him, gripping his bare arms with her hands. There go the hairs on my neck, again. He is facing the crowd, with his hands out toward them. I see Rainie's hands start to glow, and she sends the flames down Ches's arms to his fingertips. I guess he doesn't have an immunity problem like Match does. When the flames reach his fingers he starts to move. He's making pictures with the flames, or spelling out words. I can't really tell. He starts to rap along with his movements. I can't look away. It's ... incredible.

People are humming and clapping in time with him. When he slows down, other people break in, rapping, singing. Someone starts to dance. The crowd makes room. At this point, Rainie has let go of Ches. She's standing next to me, picking food off my plate. We lean back against the wall and take it all in. She whispers in my ear, "Isn't the energy in here amazing?"

"Amazing." I say, hooking my arm around hers. I pass her the plate, and she takes a turn holding it, while I help myself to a chicken wing.

The afternoon goes on with more of the same, singing, dancing, eating. I'm introduced to friends and relatives. I think I've had hugs from more people in the past two hours than I've had in a year. At around three in the afternoon, my dad signals to me that it's time to go. I point to the hallway to let him know I'm going to use the bathroom first. Rainie comes with me.

The wall in the hallway is covered with photographs. Rainie and I stop to look. Most of the pictures are of Match, Ches, and Jazz. Some are with their grandmother. But in a few, we see a younger woman … Match's mom?

"Do you know what happened to her?" Rainie asks me.

I shake my head. "He's never mentioned her," I say.

We move down the hall. There are two doors. I peek into one, and see a double bed and dresser. Grandma's room? The other door is the bathroom. Rainie and I go in together.

"I don't get it," I say. "Where are the other bedrooms?"

"I guess there aren't any," she says.

When we get back out front, my dad and Harm are by the door, saying their good-byes to Match and his grandmother. We go in for another round of hugs, expressing our deep appreciation for the hospitality, especially the food. We are about to make our exit when the door opens, and the woman from the photographs walks in.

Rainie and I lock eyes. Now what?

The woman heads straight for Match.

"My baby!" she says. "Happy Birthday, baby!"

Match stiffens, as his mom takes him into her arms. Jazz and Ches come running over.

"Mama!" they yell and jump onto the pile.

We stand there awkwardly. We've already said good-bye to everyone else, but it seems like the polite thing to wait and be introduced. Or should we back out quietly and leave them to their reunion?

Match's grandmother saves us.

"Janice. Janice! Let me introduce you to Match's friends from Fluidity."

"From where?"

"His school. In Darwin. Remember?"

She turns around to look at us. Her eyes are bloodshot.

"Darwin, huh. Well that explains the car out front. It sure don't belong to anyone who lives here," she says.

I can feel my face turn bright pink. My dad takes his cue.

"It's lovely to meet you, Janice. I'm sorry that we can't stay longer, but I'm afraid you're right, the car is waiting for us. Louise, thank you again. We had a wonderful time."

With that, we retreat into the hallway.

"See you Monday," I say to Match as the door swings shut.

"Wow, she was drunk off her—" Harm starts, but a sharp look from my dad quiets him.

Drunk? What? How could he tell? We only saw her for two minutes. When we get outside, the town car is waiting by the curb. The driver whisks us away, and we watch the scenery fly by again, this time in reverse. By the time we are back in my dad's neighborhood, with all the taxicabs, doormen, and people in spandex walking their dogs, our time in the Meadow seems like a dream. Or maybe this is the dream?

My dad invites us to stay at his place for dinner, but Harm says he needs to get the car back, so we say good-bye to my dad in the lobby. As he hugs me, he leans toward my ear and whispers, "I'm very glad I got to meet your friends, Celeste. Let's talk soon. I love you, sweetie."

"I love you, too, Dad," I say, and I give him an extra squeeze.

The drive home in the Prius is quiet. I don't know about Harm and Rainie, but I'm on sensory overload from the afternoon, so I'm thankful for the time just to sit and process my thoughts. I learned more about Match and his family today than I have all summer, but I still have so many questions. How long has he lived with his grandmother? Why does he live there and not with his mother? And, the most confusing puzzle of all for my logical brain ... where in the world in that tiny apartment does everybody sleep?

Somewhere along the way I must have fallen asleep because, the next thing I know, we are pulling into the Langfords' driveway. I get out and thank Harm for the ride. He says, "no sweat," and goes inside, leaving me and Rainie standing in the driveway.

"Wow. That was intense." she says.

"Yeah. Did you see Match when she walked in? He completely froze."

"I know. I wonder if he knew she was coming."

"It was nice to meet his brother and sister though. You and Ches seemed to get along." I stare at the ground as I say this.

She laughs.

"I can't believe it. Swergie, are you ... jealous?"

With that, my face turns bright red.

"What? Why would I be jealous? I'm just saying that was a pretty neat trick you did with the flames and everything. Why would I—"

"Swergie. Relax," she says. "I think I like it."

She leans in and gives me a kiss on the cheek. My skin burns at the touch of her lips.

"Talk to you tomorrow?" she asks.

"Yeah. Tomorrow."

"Great."

She heads for the door, and I cross the street to my house.

Layla ambushes me the minute I walk in. "Come upstairs, immediately," she says. "I need a full debriefing."

"I'll be right up," I say.

I cut through the kitchen where my mom and Jackie are making dinner.

"There she is," says my mom, smiling. "How was the party?"

"It was great," I say. "Um, did anyone call while I was gone?"

She frowns. "No, sweetie, I'm sorry. Were you expecting to hear from someone?"

"Not exactly. I just thought May might be home this weekend."

I head up the back stairs, then up to Layla's room. She's typing into her phone, but she stops when she sees me.

"Well, tell me about it," she says. "I cannot believe Dad let you do that. And I can't believe I didn't get to go! Harm better not have been flirting with any girls. I told him you would tell me everything, so—"

"So, do you want me to tell you, or what?"

"Yeah, yeah, go ahead."

I do my best to capture the feeling of the party, the food, the music, the people. I tell her about the awkward run-in with Match's mom. I leave out a few little details, like my reaction to Ches and Rainie, and Rainie's kiss in the driveway. I wouldn't know what to say about that anyway, since I don't understand it myself. Layla listens, which is a miracle, and after I'm done, I ask her to tell me about her meet. Before we know it, it's time for dinner. We go downstairs, arm in arm, and I'm pretty sure I'll remember this as one of the best days of my life.

39

Monday morning, we are back at Fluidity. As we file out of morning meeting, Rainie and I are wandering over to the pond, as usual, when I see Match heading for the garden.

"Rainie, um, I think I'm gonna weed this morning."

She looks at me, then at Match, who is almost out of sight by the barn.

"Okay," she says with a smile. "I'll catch up with you at yoga."

When I get to the garden, Match is already halfway down his first row. I grab a wheelbarrow and head down the row next to him. He looks up when he hears the wheelbarrow rumbling down the aisle.

"Hey," he says.

"Hey."

He goes back to weeding, and I fall in behind him, cleaning up the mess he leaves behind. By now, he knows which ones are weeds. I think he just doesn't care. At least, today he doesn't.

"What did those carrots ever do to you?" I ask, jokingly.

"What?"

"I said, 'what did those carrots ever do to you?'"

"I heard what you said. I just don't get it."

"You know, you're ripping those carrots out of the ground like you have it out for them, that's all."

He looks down at his hand, which holds an indiscriminate mix of carrot tops and weeds.

"I don't belong here," he says.

"Don't say that. You just have to be more careful, that's all."

"Not here in the garden, Celeste. I mean, here. Here. Are you blind? I don't belong here."

"Match, what are you talking about? Of course you belong here. You're—"

"What? A freak? Like the rest of you? This is freak camp, right? You all think you have it so tough. *'I don't know what I am, so I have to go to private school and swim and play all day.'* This is such a joke. I should be home looking after my brother and sister. I don't know why I thought you people could change anything."

I'm officially speechless. I have never heard him talk this much. Or sound this angry. He's supposed to be my voice of reason. The calm, cool one.

"Match, I'm sorry …"

He looks at me, and he snaps back into focus.

"Don't be sorry, C. I don't mean you. I just want to get my sister and brother out of there so bad, and I can't. I came here to help them, and instead, it's like … it's like I left them, just like everybody else."

"Everybody else? You mean your mom?"

No answer.

"You didn't leave them. They know that. They know."

Because the silence is killing me, and because I don't know what else to say, I blurt out the first thing that comes to mind.

"Match, can I ask you a personal question?"

"Sure. What?"

"Um, where do you sleep, exactly?"

He gives me one of his famous Match smirks.

"Why? You goin' all stalker on me?"

I blush. "No. I just … I only saw one bedroom in your grandmother's apartment … never mind. You don't have to tell me."

"No, it's a'ight. My grandma and Jazz share the bedroom. Ches and I sleep on the foldout couch."

"Oh, okay."

"Anything else you want to ask me?"

So many things.

"One more thing. Your mom. I'm sorry if this is a horrible thing to ask, but … why don't you live with her?"

He looks at me, and I know I've pushed him as far as he'll go.

"Mmm. We're better off with my grandma, that's all."

I nod and turn back to my weeding. Match does the same. A little while later, he starts to sing, "Ain't No Sunshine When She's Gone." I close my eyes and listen.

40

I'm hugging a purple velvet pillow, smoothing the fabric down in one direction until it's all silky and shiny, then rubbing it the other way so that the fuzz stands on end. Dr. Metzger lets me do this for a good five minutes before she breaks the silence.

"This weekend was the birthday party, wasn't it?"

"Mm hmm."

"Did you go to Match's house?"

"Mmm. His apartment. In the Meadow."

"What was that like?"

"Small."

"The apartment was small?"

"Yeah. It only had one bedroom for four people."

"I see."

"We got to meet Match's brother and sister … and his mom, I guess."

"You guess?"

"She doesn't live with him. She just sort of showed up as we were leaving. I don't think Match even knew she was coming. Can you imagine not even knowing if your mom is coming to your birthday party?"

"That must be difficult for him."

"I guess so. He doesn't like to talk about it."

I go back to massaging the pillow. There is silence again.

This time, I am the one to break it.

"This is so stupid."

"What is so stupid?"

I look around.

"This. All of this. This pillow. Those stupid lava lamps. Everything about this. It isn't real."

"This room doesn't feel real to you?"

"Not this room. This ... life. My life."

"Your life doesn't feel real?"

"I don't even know what I'm doing here. I don't have any problems. I have parents. I have two ridiculous houses. Match and his brother sleep on a foldout couch every night. Jazz and Ches have to drop out of school, and I'm complaining because I might have to go to private school? I hate myself."

"It's natural to wish that your friends could have the advantages that you have. Why does that make you hate yourself?"

"Because ... because it does. I have all these things, and I'm not happy. I don't deserve any of it."

"What would make you deserving of your life?"

"I don't know. Nothing."

"This weekend you came face to face with some very grown-up realities. One of which is that not every family is as well off as your own. A great many, in fact, are not."

"Why is it that way? Don't people care?"

"I think many people care, Celeste. You, for one."

"So what? So what if I care? What good does that do?"

"Well, caring is the first step to acting."

"Mmm."

I study my sandals for a minute.

"Um, Dr. M?"

"Yes."

Rainie kissed my cheek, and it sent goosebumps up my spine.

"Nothing."

41

Another week goes by, and I'm in the pavilion, face down in child's pose, when I feel a tap on my shoulder. It's Liz, the camp director. She brings me to the main office where my mom is waiting. My mom's eyes are red and puffy. Why is she crying now?

"Everything's okay," she says.

Now I know things are not okay.

"What is it?" I ask. "What happened?"

"It's May," she says. "She's going to be fine, but she's in the hospital."

"What? Why? Was she in an accident?"

"Not an accident," she says. "Poison ivy."

For a moment, I can't speak. My mind has to wrap around what I'm hearing. "Poison ivy," I say. "But Earths don't get …"

Oh, May.

"She's been sent home from Gray Rock," my mom says. "And, of course, unless something changes, she won't be eligible for DES this fall. Mrs.

Jacobs asked if we could drop by the hospital to see her. Apparently, she's been pretty depressed since she got back." *Since she got back?* How long has she been here? And why didn't she call me?

I guess I know why.

I'm scared and angry and sad, all at once. Most of all, I just don't understand.

"But, mom, I still don't get why she's in the hospital. Even if she's not an Earth, it's just poison ivy. Is there something else?"

My mom won't meet my gaze. "Let's worry about that later. I told Mrs. Jacobs we'd be at the hospital at noon. May can tell you more, if she's up to it."

We ride the rest of the way to the hospital in silence.

May's parents are in the hallway outside her room, talking to a doctor. They appear tired, wrinkled, and sad. Their resigned look tells me that whatever tears they have shed over what's happening, it was days ago. When they see us, they attempt to smile and wave us over.

Mrs. Jacobs turns to my mom and says, "Lena, thank you so much for being here." Then she looks at me, "Celeste, I know it means so much to May that you're here. Why don't you go in? She's waiting for you."

May is sitting up in the bed when I walk in. When I first see her, I have to work to hide my shock. Half of her face is covered in bandages. There are large bandages on both of her calves and one of her forearms. She uses her unbandaged arm to pick up the remote control and turn off the TV. I steady myself with the back of a chair.

"You should sit down," she says. "You look like you might faint."

I sit.

"It's really not as bad as it looks," she continues. "They just put these bandages on me because they're worried about infection."

"Infection? From the poison ivy?" I ask.

"Well, that and …"

"That and what?"

"CJ … I'm … really glad you're here. I wasn't sure you'd come, with everything that happened."

"I will always be here for you, May. You're my best friend, no matter what."

"Will you keep visiting me then?"

"How long will you be here?"

"Until the weekend, I think. The cuts have to heal, and they have to be sure—"

"Cuts?"

"—that I'm not going to … do anything else."

"May, what are you talking about? I don't understand."

"I cut myself, CJ."

"Cut yourself, how?"

"I wasn't trying to hurt myself, I swear. I just wanted to get rid of the poison ivy. I thought if I could hide it, or get rid of it, no one would have to know."

"May—"

"No, just listen to me. It wasn't supposed to get this out of hand. I had a few spots of poison ivy on my leg, and I thought if I just scraped them off, that would be it. One of the older girls at camp had a razor that she used to shave her legs, so I borrowed it. I pretended I was really bad at it because it was my

182

first time and all. It was just a couple of scrapes on my legs. But the rash didn't go away. It just kept spreading. I didn't know what else to do. I couldn't tell anyone. I knew if they found out they would send me home. And my parents ... they were so excited when I got in to Gray Rock. I didn't want to disappoint them."

"May, I don't know what to say."

"Don't say anything then. Just sit here with me, okay? If I have to watch another soap opera, I swear I'm gonna barf."

With that, we both start laughing. She doesn't mention the thing with Rainie, and I don't bring it up. Instead, we just chat about TV shows, clothes, movies, all the stuff we used to talk about.

I feel a hole in my heart start to fill again.

42

"Hey, where have you been?" asks Rainie, when I get to camp late the next morning. "I was starting to worry about you."

She looks up at me from her sketch book, smiling. I've been dreading this moment, but it seems like no matter what I do, someone's going to hate me.

"I went to see May. She's in the hospital."

Rainie visibly bristles at May's name.

"What happened? Is she all right?"

"She's okay. She's getting better. She's just stuck there for a few more days."

"Oh. Good. I mean, as long as she's going to be okay, I can go back to despising her."

"She's not a bad person," I try, although I'm not sure why I think this will have any effect.

"Oh, no. She doesn't mean any harm. She just thinks they should lock me up for my own good, right?"

"She never said that. Anyway, I don't expect you to understand, but she's my best friend, and I'm going to be there for her."

This hits Rainie like a slap in the face.

"Your best friend. Right. I keep forgetting I'm just filler, until the real thing gets back."

She leaves her sketch pad in the grass and starts walking toward the goat barn.

"Rainie, wait! That's not fair. I never said you weren't my friend, too. I just can't abandon her right now. She needs me."

"Why? What's the matter with her?"

"I can't tell you. I promised her I wouldn't tell anyone."

"Oh, I see. So you can tell her my most personal stuff—without even asking me, I might add—but you can't tell me a thing about her? That sounds fair."

We reach the barn. She goes inside and starts to drag the food around for the goats. It's a bucket full of scraps from the kitchen. It reeks. She heaves it into the trough and heads back to the barn for more.

"I couldn't ask you because you weren't even talking to me then, remember? Anyway, her thing's more serious. I mean, she's in the hospital for chrissake, Rainie!"

She looks up from the bucket she's dragging, and her green eyes are bright with tears.

"I'm sorry," she says. "It's just that it feels like it's all happening again. Every time I start to trust this … trust you … it feels like I'm losing you. To her. Again."

I walk up to her, take the bucket from her hands and set it down by the fence. I reach up. My fingers curl around the back of her neck, as my thumbs wipe the tears from her cheeks.

"Rainie," I whisper, "you're not going to lose me. She's just a friend. You are … you are …"

I'm not really sure who starts it. All I know is that we're kissing. My first real kiss. She is kissing me, and I'm kissing her. Her lips are the softest thing I have ever felt. I want to live in this moment, forever.

Then she breaks away. Suddenly, I'm full of doubt. Was she kissing me back? I don't know anymore. I can't look at her. What if she is disgusted by me? What if she hates me? "I'm sorry," I say, and I run, head down, towards the office. She calls after me, but I am gone. So gone.

43

My mom comes to pick me up, no questions asked. By the time we get home, I'm crying inconsolably. She takes me up to my bed. She sits next to me, rubs my back and whispers that it'll be okay. She does this until the sobbing subsides. When my breathing finally returns to normal, she asks me, "Celeste, sweetie, can you tell me what's wrong?"

"I ... I ..." the sobbing is starting to return, so I stuff my face back in the pillow and let it out.

"It's okay. Just try to breathe. You don't have to talk."

"Mom, ... I ... I ... think I ... kissed Rainie," I manage between sobs.

If she's surprised, she doesn't show it. She just keeps rubbing my back.

"Sweetie, I'm glad—"

"You're glad!" I scream at her. "About what? About the fact that no matter what I do, I will never be normal, EVER?" I can hardly contain the anger in my voice. She can't look me in the face and tell me that this is a good thing. She's always turning things around on me.

"I'm glad that you have the courage to follow your heart." she says, calmly. "If I could have done that earlier, it would have saved your father and me a lot of heartache."

This stops me in my tracks. This is the first time that she's talked to me about why she and my dad got divorced. I mean, we all know why, but she has never spoken about it directly to me or Layla before.

"Sweetie, I don't regret marrying your father, and I never will, because we had you and Layla, and you are the most important people in my life. But, at the same time, I owed it to your father to be honest with him … and myself. And if there's anything that I wish for you and your sister, and the boys, it is that you will be true to yourselves, whatever that means. Right now, you are only thirteen. You don't have to put the weight of the world on one kiss. You have time to get to know yourself and your feelings. I'm just glad that your heart is open."

I don't speak. I can't.

"Celeste," she goes on, "I know it's been especially hard for you … having Jackie around. And I don't know if I can communicate to you what it means to me to have her and the boys in our lives. All I can say is that I get the same feeling from being in this house with our family, our whole family, that I get from being in my garden. It fills me with life. If it's possible, I have even more love to give you and Layla, because I'm receiving so much love. Does that make sense?"

Not totally, but I nod anyway. I guess I get the picture. She loves Jackie. Jackie loves her. They love us. It's a love fest.

"Thanks, mom," I say, and I close my eyes. I don't think I can take any more big revelations right now. I just want to sleep.

"I love you," she says. She gives me a kiss on the forehead and leaves me to my nap.

44

My mom lets me stay home from camp for the rest of the week. I lie low and watch more TV than is probably healthy. I only surface to visit with May in the afternoons.

Her bandages are off now. She's right that it's not as bad as I imagined. She has a scar on her right cheek that, strangely, reminds me of the flag of Texas, and some smaller, non-descript scars on her forearm, shins, and calves.

Every now and then, I see glimpses of the old May, like when she charms the kitchen staff into bringing an extra dessert for me to eat, but there's a sadness below the surface that wasn't there before.

Finally, on the afternoon before her discharge, I tell her about Rainie and the kiss. A smile creeps across her face, and I see the old glint in her eyes. "CJ, I've known since that night in the club, probably longer."

"What do you mean 'since that night in the club'? I just kissed her four days ago."

"I don't mean about the kiss. I mean about you. That was when I saw you with Match and Harm, remember? Those two are beyond hot! If you haven't been lusting after them since day one of camp, you definitely do NOT like boys. I have to admit though, you and Match almost threw me off with that kiss. But, looking back, it's obvious you were just overcompensating."

"Oh, really?" I smile. "That's a pretty big word. Been spending time with a psychiatrist much? Anyway, I'm glad to hear you have it all figured out. I'm gonna need a little more time, okay?"

"Whatever. Just let me know when you catch up."

God, I've missed her confidence. I've missed my friend.

"So," I say, "what are you going to do once you're out of here?"

"Um, about that …"

May tells me that her parents have been struggling with what to do with her. They don't want her back in Medley Camp, pretty much for the same reasons my mom didn't want me there. They also don't want her spending too much time at home alone. After talking with my mom, May's parents have decided that the best thing for her would be to spend as much time as possible surrounded by friends, in a low-pressure, non-judgmental environment.

That's right, come Monday morning, May Jacobs is coming to Fluidity Camp with me.

45

I decide Rainie deserves a little warning. Besides, I have to face her at some point, and maybe it's better if it's not in the middle of morning meeting.

It's Sunday night. The lights are on in the Langfords' living room, so I ring the bell. Harm answers. He can't help giving me a knowing smile when he sees me. "Hey, Celeste. Here to see Rainie?"

"Yeah. Thanks."

He tilts his head back into the house. "Rainie, it's your ... *friend*, Celeste."

Jerk.

Rainie comes to the door, and we go outside together. Harm lingers in the doorway a little too long.

"Get lost!" orders Rainie.

"Okay, okay." He smiles and shuts the door.

"Let me guess. He knows."

"Uh huh. Sorry he's acting so weird. You have your sister to talk to. I've got him."

"What did you tell him, exactly?"

"Just, you know, that we kissed." *We kissed.* I breathe an inner sigh of relief. At least she isn't disgusted by me.

"So, that was ... okay ... with you?"

"A little more than okay, Swergie," she says, and she reaches out for my hand.

I blush and break eye contact.

Now, for the really hard part.

"Um, Rainie?"

"Yeah?"

"There's something else I have to tell you ..."

She takes it pretty well. When I tell her about May's reaction to our kiss, it warms her up a little; she even cracks a smile. At the end she says, "Fine, I can deal with her, for you, but that doesn't mean I have to like it."

Okay, I've done what I can. I just have to cross my fingers that the rest will work itself out. That, and come to morning meeting prepared to break up a catfight. Yeah, I'm pretty much counting on a catfight.

46

My mom and I pick up May on the way to camp. She's wearing jeans and a long-sleeved lavender tee shirt. Her hair is down. The scar on her cheek comes in and out of view as she moves. It is SO obvious she is trying to hide her scars. I mean, jeans, for chrissake. It's going to be eighty degrees out. Anyway, good luck hiding it when you have the flag of Texas on your face.

I'm a jerk.

In the car, I prep her for what camp has in store. Morning meeting. Chanting. Contribution Chart. Cow bell. She listens closely and doesn't crack a smile. She's nervous. Old May has gone out the window again.

We enter the meeting house and everyone turns to look. At least that's the way it feels. I spot Rainie, Match, and Harm and head over to them.

"Hi guys, you remember May?"

There's a round of awkward "hellos," or in Match's case, a simple nod, then we sit. No one speaks. *Please, start the meeting.* I telepathically plead with Liz. Then, without a word, Match extends his huge hand toward May's face. She's startled; I can see her eyeing the matchstick tattoo, but she stays put. With a gentle caress, he pulls the hair back from her face and says, "Nice scar. You should tattoo it ... when you're old enough."

I see the old May sparkle ignite, and she says, "What makes you think I'm not old enough now?"

Oh, brother.

In my peripheral vision, I see Rainie's eyes roll. But at least the old May is back. Thank you, Match.

During morning meeting, May is called to stand up. Oops. I forgot to warn her about that part. But by then, she's back to being old May, so she soaks up the attention, giving the crowd her best beauty-queen wave. The effect is immediate. By the end of the meeting, people I've never met before are coming up to her. "May, remember I played on your soccer team in third grade?" "May, remember we used to have the same dentist?" "May, remember you dropped your gum on the sidewalk once, and I stepped in it?"

Rainie is about to start flaming any minute, and even I am a little annoyed at this point. I mean, where were all these people on my first day? But it's not May's fault. Some people just have "it," and she's one of them.

Rainie, May, and I head over to the Contribution Chart, and with a little behind-the-scenes prodding on my part, Rainie rigs it so the three of us are on dishes together. Lunch seems like a year from now. I still have hours to keep these two from pulling each other's hair out.

I suggest sketch pads down by the pond, and we all settle into a shady spot next to Willow. May and I are debating the fine points of the dress on the latest cover of *Teen Earth*, when Rainie abruptly gets up and says she forgot that she promised Hope she would cover for her on goat duty today. Before either of us can respond, she's headed up the hill toward the barn.

"Was it something I said?" asks May. When Rainie is out of sight, May turns to me and asks, "She hates me, doesn't she?"

"Um, I don't know if hate is the right word," I say.

"Well, something's going on. She hasn't looked me in the eye once since I got here."

"This is just a guess, but it could have something to do with the fact that you said she needed to be fixed."

"You told her that?"

"Yeah, I told her. That was an insane thing to say, May."

"Oh my God, no wonder she hates me."

"I told you, she doesn't hate you. She's just … mad. I thought maybe she was over it, but …"

"What should I do?"

"An apology would be good. Just, um, hang back a little when you do it."

"Hang back?"

"You know, in case it gets heated."

"Heated. Right. Thanks."

The only problem is, we don't see Rainie again for the rest of the day. She even misses lunch, which is pretty unheard of. She must have told someone she's sick and gone home. Or hidden in the meeting house.

Sometimes they'll let you eat lunch late if you're deep in meditation when the bell rings.

I'm busy showing May around, so I have to admit, I don't look all that hard for Rainie. In fact, I'm a little pissed off at her. She promised me she would make an effort with May here, and she lasted all of one hour. Some effort.

May and I make the best of it. I give her the "Greatest Hits" tour of Fluidity: yoga with Shanti, musically-assisted cleanup with Nona, and storytelling with Ben. I do my best to have a good time, but it just doesn't feel right without Rainie.

As the day goes on, I realize something. May is a natural at yoga. May is a natural at musically-assisted cleanup. May is a natural at storytelling. The truth is, there's not much May doesn't do well. Putting myself in Rainie's shoes, I have to admit that if May wasn't already my best friend, I would probably find it annoying. But how can I be annoyed with her for just being good at stuff? Besides, this never bothered me before. In fact, I admired her for it.

By the end of the day, my mood is in the toilet. To sum up: I'm pissed off at Rainie, annoyed with May, and pretty disgusted with myself for feeling that way.

This day sucks.

At home that night, I can't face the prospect of sitting at the dinner table, answering all the inevitable questions: "How was camp today?" "What did you do?" "Was it all sunshine and roses having May there with you?" So I tell my mom I'm not feeling well, and I head off to bed with a couple of granola bars stashed in my pockets. At least the day is over.

If only I didn't have to do it all over again tomorrow.

47

The next day, I'm actually relieved to have my appointment with Dr. Metzger. I settle into the purple velvet and close my eyes. For about five minutes, no one speaks. Finally, it is Dr. Metzger who breaks the silence.

"How is camp going now that May is there with you?" she asks.

Right to point, as always, eh, Dr. M?

"It sucks," I say, equally to the point.

"How so?"

I explain my newfound annoyance with May's perfection, Rainie's refusal to accept May, everything.

Dr. Metzger is silent for a minute.

"Have you tried putting yourself in May's place?"

"What place?"

"I mean, have you tried to imagine what it felt like for her to lose her identity, to lose Gray Rock?"

"But I never even had that to begin with, so how can she be—"

"We're not talking about you right now."

We're not? Oh, yeah.

"Well, I know it must have been hard, but—"

"Why is there a 'but' attached to that?"

"I just mean, now that she's back, why does she have to be so—"

"Before you start debating whether May 'should' be thinking and feeling and doing the things that annoy you, why don't you spend some time trying to understand *why* she might be thinking and feeling and doing those things."

Argh. Sometimes introspection is so annoying.

"Fine. So it's all *my* fault, is that it?"

"I never said anything about fault. I just think it might help you to be more mindful of what other people might be feeling. It could help you understand their actions better."

Mindful. Seems like my mind is plenty full as it is.

I am so wiped out by the time I leave my appointment that I spend the car ride home staring out the window like a zombie. My mom takes pity on me and lets me stay home the rest of the day. When evening comes, I ask if she will take me over to May's house. She calls May's parents, who say that I am welcome to stop by for a visit before dinner.

May meets me at the door. She's in jeans again, even though it must have been near ninety degrees today. Her hair is down.

We go to her room and sit down opposite each other on the rug. She leans back against the edge of her bed. May's fern, a constant at her bedside, is missing. In fact, looking around, I notice that all the plants have been removed from her room.

"What happened to Fern?" I ask.

"She's in the living room," says May. "My parents decided I need a break from, you know, thinking about all that stuff."

"Oh," I say. "Do you miss her?"

"Yeah, but I still see her every day. It's just, I don't have to, like, think about whether she's noticing me or not. … Are you feeling okay? You weren't at camp today."

"I'm okay. I had my appointment in the morning, and I guess I just didn't feel like going after."

"It was lonely there without you."

"Well, now you know how I felt the whole time without you here."

I see the words sting her.

"I'm sorry," I say. "I'm trying not to do that anymore."

"Why are you so mad at me?" she asks.

"I'm not mad at you, I swear. I'm just … I'm … okay, maybe, I was a little pissed at you yesterday. Why is everything always so easy for you? I've been there all summer, and I've barely made three friends. You are there five minutes and everyone is fawning all over you."

"Easy? You call getting kicked out of camp, ending up in the hospital, losing all my new friends and my boyfriend, easy? You are really messed up, you know that? Now I'm covered in scars that will never go away. I'm always going to be reminded of what a stupid idiot I am—"

"May, you are not stupid. I had no idea you were feeling this way. I—"

"How could you not know? All those days that you visited me at the hospital, did you ever once see Noah or any of the other GR people there? I didn't even get a card or a text from Noah. It's like I don't even exist for him anymore."

"May, I'm so sorry. You're better than they are."

"I know you never liked Noah. But it still hurts, CJ. And now that I'm finally starting to feel better again, you're mad at me. For what? For being me?"

"I know. I'm not mad at you, really. I'm mad at myself. You, you are amazing. I can't even believe all the stuff you've been through this summer. And even then, it's like, you're a star, no matter where you are. It's fantastic. I'm so jealous I could spit in your beautiful, scarred face."

She laughs.

"Don't you *dare*. I will totally tear your hair out."

She puts up one hand like a tiger's claw and does a half-hearted little roar.

I start cracking up.

"Oh my God, May, I missed you so much this summer."

"Me, too."

"Could you do me a favor, though?"

"What?"

"Cut it out with the jeans, would you? You must be sweating your butt off."

"Is it that obvious? I am so hot! I just wish fall would hurry up and get here already."

"Why are you so worried about your scars? We already know one person who likes them."

She blushes.

"What is the deal with you and Match, anyway?" she asks, looking down at the carpet.

"No deal. We're just friends. Really."

"So, you won't be mad if I tell you that I kind of like him?"

I feign surprise.

"What? You like Match? I would never have guessed that in a million years."

She smiles.

"You are a real jerk, you know that, Jardine?"

"I know. It's my specialty, apparently."

"I love you, CJ."

"I love you, too, Maysie."

We stand up and hug.

"See you tomorrow?" she asks.

"You bet."

Now we just have to get Rainie on board. Good luck with that.

48

The next day at morning meeting, Rainie is there, sitting in her usual spot next to Harm and Match. When May and I walk over, I can see her heat up, even though we haven't even said anything yet.

When the meeting lets out, Rainie walks fast for the door. May and I catch up to her outside, on the path to the kitchen.

"Rainie, STOP!" I yell. "You can't keep avoiding us forever."

"Forever?" she mimics. "It's been less than forty-eight hours, Swergie. Not exactly forever."

"Whatever," I say. "Can you just stop and listen? May has something she wants to say."

I look at May. She's looking a little tongue-tied. It looks like Superman has found her Kryptonite. She's withering in Rainie's emerald green gaze.

"May," I prompt. "Tell Rainie what you were telling me the other day ... about being sorry for what you said."

"What's the matter?" Rainie asks May, "Did you forget your lines?"

"What is the point of this, CJ?" May says to me. "It's pretty clear she hates me, and nothing I say is going to change that."

"May, how would you know that? You haven't even said anything yet … and Rainie, do me a favor, just shut up and listen for a minute," I shout. Now both of them are staring at me, as is the growing crowd of Fluidity campers that has accumulated on the path.

May turns to Rainie, "I'm sorry," she says. "I'm sorry for what I said about you needing a doctor. I'm sorry for telling Noah and his friends about you. I'm sorry for everything. I had just never met anyone … like you. I think in my heart I thought I was trying to help."

"Well, I don't need your help—"

"I know that now, okay? I don't know what else I can say."

"Do you want to be here, May?" Rainie asks abruptly.

"What?" asks May, looking confused.

"Do you want to be here, at Fluidity? Because I do. I've grown up with this place, and if you and I are going to get along, you have to learn to respect that … to respect what this place is about."

"Have I done something that makes you think I don't?"

"You haven't done anything, exactly. It's just … I don't know, your attitude. You waltz in here like you own the place, and you don't even know anything about it." Now she turns to me. "And you're not exactly helping, Swergie. Spoon-feeding everything to her."

"How is that any different from what you did for me?" I ask.

She pauses. "You know what? You're right. It's time for something that is long overdue. Come on … both of you."

"What are you talking about?" I ask. "What's long overdue?"

"Your initiation."

She leads us over the hill to the goat barn. The crowd of Fluidity campers follows. Apparently, this is much more exciting than whatever self-exploration activities they had planned.

We all gather around Rainie at the entrance to the barn. "Okay," she says. "If you really want to be a part of this place, you can't go around cherry-picking jobs anymore." This one is directed at me. My face flushes. Guilty, as charged. May looks at me, questioningly. I shrug.

"That's why, this morning, both of you are going to milk a goat."

The Fluidity crowd is eating this up. There's a whistle and a cheer from somewhere. I see Match and Harm at the back, laughing their butts off.

May and I look at each other. I'm trying to gauge whether she's actually going to go through with this. But, looking at her now, there is no way she will back down. The audience is pumping her up. All the attention fuels her like gasoline. I wish it had that effect on me. All it's done for me so far is make my palms sweaty.

Rainie takes Melanie from the pen and leads her to a raised platform inside the barn with some sort of wooden contraption at the front for Melanie to poke her head through. Rainie fills a bucket with grain and sets it in front of Melanie's head. She turns back towards us.

"This is Melanie's udder," Rainie says, pointing at the huge, bulging sack hanging between Melanie's back legs.

How does she even walk with that thing? It must weigh a ton. Judging by the size, there must be a gallon of milk in there, at least. I imagine carrying a gallon jug of milk around suspended between my legs, then quickly banish the thought.

Rainie washes Melanie's udder with a wet rag. "These are her teats," she says, pointing at the two nipples, the size of thumbs, hanging down, one on each side of the udder. At least there are only two of them, I think. Rainie dries the teats with another rag, then grabs a small bowl from the shelf. "The first few squeezes we don't keep," she says. I watch as she sprays some milk from each teat into the bowl and sets it aside.

"Now it's your turn," she says to me, placing a large bucket under the udder. Oh, Melanie, I apologize in advance for what I'm about to do. I sit down in the chair and look up at Rainie, blankly.

"Okay, Swergie, there's nothing to it. Wrap your thumb and forefinger, tightly, around the base of the teat to trap the milk in, then squeeze the milk out into the bucket with your other fingers. Whatever you do, don't pull down. It'll hurt her and damage her udder."

Damage? Oh, dear God, I don't want to have udder damage on my hands. I reach out my hand and grab one teat, as gently as I can. I give it a squeeze or two. Nothing comes out. Melanie's lifts one of her back legs, knocking it into my hand. I pull my hand away.

"Don't let her put you off," says Rainie. "Just leave your hand there, firmly but gently. You're not squeezing tightly enough at the top."

After a few more tries, I get into a rhythm, and the milk is flowing. I can't believe I'm actually doing this! May has been watching me, so by the time she sits down to take my place, she's practically a pro compared to me, with only a few false starts and nervous giggles. At the end, Rainie dips Melanie's teats in some solution, and we're done.

I know that all we did was milk a goat, but the adrenaline is coursing through me like I just stared down a grizzly bear. Rainie puts the milk away and returns Melanie to her pen, and the three of us walk out of the barn to a huge round of applause from the other campers. We oblige with a wave, then head off toward our usual spot by the pond.

"That was unbelievable!" I say, to no one in particular.

"I know," May agrees, "I can't believe I just did that. I swear, I thought Melanie was going to kick me halfway through!"

"You did great," says Rainie. She pauses, then adds, "both of you."

She and May look at each other. Something passes between them … a truce, maybe.

"We still have a problem," says May, although she's smiling as she says it.

"What is it?" I ask.

"What are we going to do about your nickname? All this CJ/Swergie stuff is confusing me."

"That's easy," says Rainie. "Swergie is way cooler than CJ."

"But CJ is prettier."

"Who wants a 'pretty' nickname?"

"You two will find anything to fight about, you know that?" I say, but I can't help laughing. "What about Celeste?" I suggest. "That is my *name* after all."

They both look at each other for a second.

"Naaah," they say in unison.

"What about C-Swergs?"

"Eww. Ugly. Swerg-Jay?"

"Hmm. Maybe."

This goes on for a while, until I drag them to yoga, where, thankfully, there is not much talking. Frankly, I don't care what they call me, as long as they're getting along.

49

Tomorrow is my birthday. I'm lying awake in bed, wondering how this became my life. I'm not complaining. Every day I get to hang out with my best friend and my ... more-than-a-friend, and, so far, they have managed not to kill one another. So, what is there to complain about? It's just so different from the life I thought I would have. I'm letting go of source school, letting go of the idea that I can have the perfect life that everyone wants, even letting go of the idea that such a life exists. Tomorrow, my dad and all my friends are coming over, and, along with my mom, Jackie, Layla, and the boys, we will eat cake, drink lemonade, and swim in our very own, disgustingly salty pool. Things could definitely be worse.

My cell phone rings. It's my dad.

"Hi, Dad."

"Hi, sweetie, I just wanted to say good night to you on your last day of being thirteen."

"So far, I don't feel any different."

"Are you excited for tomorrow?"

"Yeah. Of course."

"I talked to your mom, and she is on board with the Paris plan. What do you say to a celebration dinner with you, me and your sister on the Eiffel Tower?"

"Dad, can I talk to you about Paris?"

"Of course, sweetie, what is it?"

"It's just ... I was hoping for something else for my birthday."

* * *

After I get off the phone with my dad, I drift off to sleep with the uncomfortable realization that, tomorrow, I will have to wear a bathing suit in front of everyone. I've grown up a lot this summer, in more ways than one. Whose bright idea was this pool party, anyway? ... Jackie. Of course ... Jackie.

"Celeste ... Celeste!"

I wake up, and I'm in her arms. Jackie's arms. She is cradling me like a child, and the fire alarm is blaring. I break away from her with a start.

"What are you doing?" I demand, still bleary-eyed.

"There's no time," she says. "Come outside, now!"

When we leave my room, I can smell the smoke. My mom is in the hall, with Matty in her arms. He's crying. "Where are Layla and Devon?" I ask.

"They're outside. Come on."

Layla and Devon are across the street on the Langfords' porch. The whole Langford family is with them. The four of us cross the street to join them. A siren wails, and a fire truck pulls up in front of our house. I take Matty into my arms, and mom and Jackie head over to talk to the firefighters.

Devon is clinging to Layla. He's wrapped in a towel, and his hair is wet. Harm and Rainie are sitting on either side of them. Harm and Layla are holding hands. I sit down next to Rainie, with Matty in my lap. Rainie puts her arm around my waist and squeezes. Layla sees this. She tries to meet my eyes, but I look away.

Harm says to Devon, "You okay, little man?"

"Yeah," squeaks Devon.

"The alarm's scary, right?" says Harm. "Do you know how many times I've set off the alarm in my house?"

"How many?" asks Devon, his interest clearly piqued.

"Twenty-seven."

"Twenty-seven!" exclaims Devon in disbelief.

"Yeah, I'm surprised the fire truck didn't just pull up in front of our house, out of habit."

Layla is eating this up. She's practically drooling. Down, girl.

"Did your mommy get mad at you?" asks Devon.

"Yeah," replies Harm. "Some of the time. But mostly, moms are just happy when everyone is okay. Do you think your mom is mad?"

"No. But she will be when she finds out."

"Finds out what?"

"That I had Albert in bed with me."

"Albert?"

"My alligator. He's not a sleep toy."

"Oh, I see. Well, even if she is a little mad, she'll get over it. We all make mistakes, little guy."

Soon, I'm going to have to get a shovel to scoop up the melted puddle of goo that is Layla.

Mom and Jackie wander back across the street and start talking to the Langfords. No, there's no real damage. Thank heaven for the early warning system. The sprinklers caught it early. We're just happy everyone is okay.

We exchange hugs with the Langfords, and we troop back over to the house. Devon's room has to be aired out and dried, so Jackie puts flame-retardant gloves on him and takes him to her and my mom's bed for the night. Matty starts to freak out that Devon gets to sleep with them and weasels his way into their bed, too. Layla goes off to dream of Harm, who has just reached god-like status in her mind. My mom comes into my room to tuck me in.

"Mom, can I talk to you about something?"

"Sure, sweetie, what is it?"

"It's just that … Jackie did something a little weird before."

"Weird?"

"Weird. Like, when she came to get me, when the alarm went off, she picked me up. I'm not exactly a kid, anymore."

"I know. She told me. I was going to wait until things settled down to talk to you about it, but—"

"Talk to me about what?"

"Celeste, she didn't pick you up—"

"She did too! I was there. She was definitely holding me. It was weird."

"I know, honey. Just let me finish. Jackie didn't pick you up. She caught you. You were levitating."

"What? No, I—"

As the words sink in, I know they're true. I also know it's not the first time. Poor Pumpkin. I could have killed him.

My mom says, "Celeste, you don't have to digest this all at once. Tonight has been very traumatic, for everyone."

"It's okay, mom. I know what I want to do."

As I say the words, I look over at my alarm clock. 12:36 a.m. It's my birthday. I'm fourteen.

50

The next morning, I'm in my room, appraising my new, fourteen-year-old bikini body. Not bad, if I do say so myself. Thank you, yoga. I throw on a flowered sundress over my bathing suit—okay, I can't say Rainie's had no effect on me—and I'm about to head downstairs when there's a knock on my door. Jackie comes in with a gift bag in her hands.

"Hi, Celeste. Your mom told me about your decision. We are both so proud of you."

"Thanks."

"Here, I wanted to give you this, before the party starts."

I take the gift bag from her. It feels like a ton of bricks. At the top of the bag, there is a box of earplugs.

"Those are earplugs," she says. Duh. "They'll help you sleep through your REM cycle. The fewer crash landings, the better, right?"

Below the earplugs, filling out the rest of the bag, is a big, purple blanket. A weighted one.

"I thought you hated these." I say.

"I don't use one," she says, a little flustered, "but I know a lot of people who swear by them. You might like it—"

"Jackie."

"I kept the receipt, so if you don't want it—"

"Jackie!"

"Sorry. What?"

"The blanket's fine. I just think … I want a tent."

She looks at me. She doesn't smile, exactly, but I can tell she is holding one back.

"Okay," she says. "I think we can manage that. Shall we head downstairs? I think the guests are starting to arrive."

"I'll be down in a minute."

After Jackie leaves the room, I stick the earplugs in my nightstand. I look at Rover, who is sitting there, motionless.

"It's okay, Rove," I say. "I know you love me."

I go out to the hall and knock on the door to the third floor.

I hear Layla say "come in," and I make the climb up to her room. She's in a bikini, too.

"I like your suit," I say. "Getting tired of racerback Speedos?"

"Yeah," she smiles. "I thought Harm might appreciate this one a little more."

"Um, are you and mom still not speaking to each other?"

"Mom and I talked last night after you went to bed," she says. "I guess we made up."

"Are you going to quit swimming?"

"No, no. Nothing like that. I'm still mad that she didn't let me go to Fluidity this summer, but it's too late for that now. Anyway, she said I don't have to try out for All Stars this year if I don't want to. That way, I won't have as many out-of-town meets. And I'll have fewer practices, so I can see Harm some during the week."

"I'm just glad you're not fighting anymore."

"Yeah. Me too. Um, Celeste?"

"Yeah?"

"Is there anything you want to ... I don't know, talk about?

"Talk about?" I know what she's asking, but I've had a few too many heart-to-hearts in the past twenty-four hours. This one will have to wait. "There's something I have to tell you," I say. "It's about France. Please don't get mad at me, okay?"

Layla takes the news better than I expected. When we are done talking, she puts her arm around me, and we head downstairs to join the party.

Outside in the yard, the sun is beating down. We are surrounded by my mom's flowers, and the new pool glistens. My dad is here ... May ... Harm, Rainie, and their parents. Even Match, Jazz, Ches, and their grandmother made it out from the city. All that anyone can talk about is the fire, Jackie discovering my levitation, and how incredible it is that this all happened the night before my birthday.

The only one who seems unimpressed is Rainie. I find her sitting on a rock in the corner of the yard, staring sullenly at her glass of lemonade.

"What's the matter, Langford?" I say. "I thought you were dying to come to one of my parties?"

Not even a smile.

"I'm sorry," she says. "I'm trying not to be selfish. I'm happy for you."

"Then what's the problem?"

"What's the problem? Seriously? After all that's happened, you have to ask that? I thought we were going to be together next year. I don't mean BE together. I just mean, go to school together ..." She's heating up. I expect a flare-up any minute.

"Whoa. Cool down, hot stuff," I say. "Who says we're not going to school together?"

"But, you said ... all you've talked about all summer is source school."

"Well, that was before I knew that my best friend and my ... you ... were going to be at Fluidity," I say. "Besides, I couldn't possibly leave now, when my work with Shanti is having such a remarkable effect." I strike a pose for her in my new bikini.

Finally, she cracks a smile.

"You mean it? You're not going to DAS?"

"Not a chance."

"Why didn't you tell me?"

"I just did. This only happened last night, remember?"

"Oh, yeah. Well, I'm glad you're staying ... obviously. I'm still going to miss you while you're in Paris though."

"Don't start missing me yet," I say.

"What do you mean by that?"

"Come on, my dad's about to explain."

I grab her hand and pull her to her feet. She gives me a squeeze and we walk hand-in-hand back toward the others.

I look at my dad and give him the signal. He taps his glass of lemonade with a spoon.

"Hello, everyone," he says. "Can I have your attention, please?"

Jackie looks questioningly at my mom. My mom shrugs. Hmm, maybe I should have given them a heads up.

My dad goes on, "We are all here today to celebrate Celeste, who is barreling towards womanhood at an alarming pace." Did he just say *womanhood*? The blood rushes to my face. Maybe I should have previewed this speech beforehand.

"And in her first act as a rebellious and independent-minded young woman of fourteen, Celeste told me last night that she wants nothing to do with the birthday trip that I had planned for her and her sister. Instead, she made a request of me. She asked me to take the money that I would otherwise have spent and create a scholarship fund for unidentified teens from the inner city to attend Fluidity. With Tyrone's permission, we'd like to name it the Matchstick Foundation. And to start it off right, we have selected two recipients of the scholarship for this coming fall term. Jasmine and Michael Robbins."

Jazz and Ches give a shout and start hugging all available bodies. Their grandmother comes up to me. She grabs my hand and pats it. "Good girl," she says. Across the patio, Match's eyes find mine. As usual, they are unreadable. Is he happy? Offended? I have no idea. I walk over to him.

"Is this okay with you?" I ask. "I'm not trying to act like I can fix everything. I know I can't just throw some money around and make everything okay. I just thought ... this would be a start, and if people see that the program is working, more people would—"

"You talk too much," he says.

"I'm working on that," I say.

He lifts me off the ground in a big bear hug.

"Don't go thinking this gets you any special treatment," he says. "You're gonna milk goats just like the rest of us."

"I wouldn't have it any other way," I say.

Rainie comes over to us. She beams at me. "Swergie, I can't believe you kept that a secret! That is unbelievable!"

Match looks at Rainie and says, "Yeah, I know one person who's gonna be real glad to go to school with you this fall," and he nods his head in Ches's direction.

Instinctively, I grab Rainie's hand. "I'm pretty sure she's not available," I say.

"For real?" he says. Rainie smiles at me and nods. A smile spreads across Match's face. He shakes his head and laughs. "A'ight. I'll be sure to let him know."

Layla is the first one to dive into the pool. She hardly makes a ripple as she breaks through the surface of the water. We all watch as she circles her way effortlessly around the bottom of the pool. She repeats the circle four or five times before surfacing.

"The water's perfect," she says. "Come on in!"

I look around at my house, my family, my friends. I may not be an Earth, but in this moment, I am shining like the sun. Everyone I care about in the entire world is here with me, and I realize, for the first time all summer, that I'm excited to start school in the fall.

ACKNOWLEDGMENTS

Thank you to everyone who offered me advice and support during this process.

To Jason Swergold, who read more drafts than anyone else and who always knew instinctively how to respond with the right ratio of encouragement and critique. You also didn't flinch when I named my thirteen-year-old, female protagonist after you.

To Allison Trzop, for being so generous with your knowledge of the publishing industry and for the title, which you handed to me on a post-it note.

To Kate Sullivan, for the best rejection ever. More than anyone else, you made me believe that this story belonged in print.

To Brent Hale, for lending your considerable design talents and for capturing the spirit of *Freak Camp* in the cover.

To Fiona and Pat Barnett-Mulligan, for that serendipitous photograph. I couldn't have staged it if I tried.

To my many volunteer readers, editors, and moral supporters, with special thanks to: Elizabeth Arnold, Eva Badway, Cristi Carman, Rosa Fox-Ogg, Bridget Miller Hale, Finlay MacNab, Kelly Matsumoto, Scott Morrissette, Marissa Peifer, Sarah Ragland, Randall Ravitz, Susanne Reardon, Argie Kosmetatos Shapiro, Anne Thomas, and last alphabetically, but far from least in contribution, Amy Venman (for those meticulous line edits).

To all my Colgate Camp readers (what a treat that was!), especially my youngest readers, Peter Treyz and Ethan Venman.

To Nataliya Urciuoli, for always setting me straight like a true friend should. ("It's a novel, not a research paper.")

To Jessica Zipkin King, for inspiring me (whether you knew it or not), by working a full-time job, parenting two young children, and still finding time to write and pursue your passion.

To Kelly Weaver, for reaching out to me and giving the book your blessing.

To my parents, Lucy Brewster and Peter and Chase Barnett, and my sister, Shelley Barnett, for your unconditional love and support in all things, this book being no exception.

To Amy Nash and Sarah Kennedy, for doing all the things that co-parents do, day in and day out.

To my sons, for giving it all meaning.

SNEAK PREVIEW OF *GIRLFLIGHT* (*FREAK CAMP*, VOL. 2):

1

Nothing in my life ever goes as planned, so why should my fourteenth birthday party be any different? My dad has just announced that my friend Match's younger sister and brother, Jazz and Ches, will be receiving scholarships to attend school at Fluidity in the fall. Fluidity is an alternative school for "unidentified" teens, meaning teens who have yet to identify their source—Earth, Air, Water, or Fire.

Not that everyone who goes to Fluidity is unidentified.

Take me, for instance. I identified as an Air this summer, so if I wanted to, I could register at the public high school for Airs in Darwin, where I live with my mom and stepmom. But by the time I identified my source, I had already made a life for myself at Fluidity. May, my best friend in the world, will be there this fall, and so will Match, one of my best friends from Fluidity Camp, who basically saved me from a summer of misery by hanging out with me when no one else would.

And then there's Rainie.

Rainie is my girlfriend. We just started going out—if you count having one real kiss and holding hands as "going out," which I definitely do. She's a Fire, which is almost unheard of for girls. That's one of the reasons she's staying at Fluidity. The idea of being the only girl at DFS—that's the public school for Fires in Darwin—did not sound very appealing to her. Besides, Rainie loves Fluidity. I totally get it. I mean, she's gone there her whole life. I'd be pretty freaked out about leaving, too, if that were me.

After the big announcement about the scholarships, the adults retreat to the shade of the screen porch, and my younger stepbrothers, Devon and Matty, go inside to watch cartoons. My sister Layla, May, and I immediately jump into the pool. The three of us are chasing each other around playing "Marco Polo," when I notice that the rest of my friends are just standing around the food table, fully dressed and bone dry, unless you count the sticky coating of sweat that is slowly seeping through their clothes.

I guess it serves me right for inviting a bunch of Fires to a pool party. Fires hate to swim, or so they say. But isn't that just another nasty stereotype? I mean, my stepbrother Devon is a Fire, and he loves to swim. Of course, he's only five years old, so maybe he's just too young to realize he's not supposed to like it. All I know is that, right now, of everyone here, only Layla (a Water), May (probably an Earth), and I (an Air) are swimming, while the rest of my friends are standing around, staring at the pool like it's some sort of swirling vortex of death. Of the non-swimmers, Rainie and her brother Harm are both fully-identified Fires, and Match and Ches both seem to be leaning that way. Could it really be just a coincidence? The only real question mark is Jazz. She at least looks curious about the water.

"Aren't you going to come in?" I shout in the general direction of the Fire crew.

"We could play volleyball in the shallow end," offers May.

Match looks at us like we've just suggested that he jump off a tall building. "I didn't bring a bathing suit," he says.

Seriously, Match? You didn't bring a bathing suit to a *pool* party? Apparently, not. And not only that, he didn't even wear shorts, which could have doubled as a bathing suit. Instead, he's sweating it out in jeans.

Of course, fitting into the crowd has never really been a priority for Match. At six feet tall, he towers over the rest of us, even Harm, who is also seventeen. Today, Match has paired his jeans with a white ribbed tank top, which contrasts with his deep brown skin and shows off his signature tattoos and burn marks. His younger brother Ches is identically dressed, minus the skin decoration. At least Rainie, Jazz, and Harm have bathing suits on, although they haven't been near the water.

"Well, we need at least one of you to make two teams for volleyball," I try.

No response.

"This is ridiculous," I say. "It's my birthday, and I demand that you all come in at least once. Harm, do you have bathing suits for Match and Ches?"

Jazz speaks up before Harm can answer. "Don't bother," she says. "I've been trying to get them to try it their whole lives. They absolutely refuse."

I stare and Match and Ches. "You mean you've *never* been swimming?" I say.

They shake their heads.

"If you saw our neighborhood pool, you'd understand why," says Match.

My cheeks flush with a now-familiar twinge of upper-middle-class shame. They must think I am the worst. I live in a huge house in Darwin, with a brand new saltwater lap pool in the back yard, and when I'm not there, I'm at my dad's swank apartment in uptown New Preston. Match, Jazz, and Ches, on the other hand, live in their grandmother's one-bedroom apartment in New Preston's run-down Meadow neighborhood. When I visited there this summer, all I could see in any direction were apartment buildings surrounded by concrete. No grass, no trees, and certainly no saltwater lap pools.

I mean, that was kind of the whole point of how I met them. Match was part of the pilot program to bring inner-city kids to Fluidity Camp, where they would be exposed to a more "natural" environment. Now that I think about it, I never did see Match go swimming in the pond at Fluidity, but he never seemed afraid of it, just disinterested.

"At least put your feet in," I say. "It's not going to hurt you."

No one moves a muscle. I'm starting to feel a good, old-fashioned temper tantrum coming on. Maybe if I start crying, they'll at least stick their feet in.

Then Jazz says, "Well, if you won't go in, I will. Unlike you all, I'm not afraid of a little water." She takes off her sandals and walks over to the stairs at the shallow end of the pool. Despite the trash talk, she looks a little nervous as she grabs the railing and dips in her first toe.

"Jazz, Jazz, Jazz," we (the swimmers) chant, as she takes another step. Now she's in up to her ankles.

"See, I told you it's not so bad," I say.

"I don't know. This feels weird," she says.

"What do you mean, weird?" asks Layla, looking up from her attempts to secure the volleyball net. Jazz takes another step, then cringes in pain.

"Aaah! What the—" she yells, as she stumbles backwards and falls down on her butt at the edge of the pool. She drags herself backwards until she's clear of the water, yelling the whole time, "Get it off me … help … it hurts … get it off!"

"Yeah, real funny," says Ches. "We get it. We're sissies, okay?"

Rainie punches Ches in the arm, "'Sissies' is offensive, you know?"

Ches laughs. "Geez, sorry."

"No, man, I think she's really hurt," says Harm.

"Get her a towel," yells Layla. "Jazz, it's going to be okay," she says. Then, to me, "Celeste, go get Dad."

For once, I don't ask why. I just run over to the porch where the grown-ups are already stirring in response to the Jazz's screams.

"Dad, help! Jazz is hurt," I say.

He and the other adults run with me to the pool. Jazz's grandmother takes Layla's place by Jazz's side. At this point, Jazz is still screaming and wiping at her feet with a towel.

"It's okay, baby. You're all right," her grandmother says.

Layla walks over to my dad and says something I can't hear. He goes over to Jazz's grandmother and asks, "Louise, has Jasmine ever been swimming in saltwater before?"

She replies, "I can't say that she has."

Jazz also shakes her head in confirmation.

"Jasmine," said my dad, "May I look at your feet?"

She nods. My dad squats down and takes one of Jazz's feet out from under the towel. He gently separates her toes, one by one, then puts her foot back down. "May I?" he asks, gesturing towards her neck. Jazz looks at her grandmother, who nods. My dad reaches forward and lifts up Jazz's hair, which hangs down in braids past her shoulders. He runs his fingers down the side of her neck, from the base of the earlobe to right above her shoulder.

"Well," he says to Jazz's grandmother, "Congratulations, she's a Water!" To Jazz, he says, "The pins-and-needles sensation you're experiencing is perfectly normal. And, I'm not a doctor, but it seems logical that there would be some additional amount of pain, considering how long these fins have been cooped up. Louise, you should make an appointment for her as soon as possible. They'll need to check out her gills to see if it's safe for her to submerge, given her, uh, late development." Well, now I know why Layla asked for him; he's a Water, just like her.

"Wait. Sub-what now?" says Jazz. "Oh, hell no! I am never going back in there."

Layla says, "Jazz, you have to—it's the best thing ever! It's not going to hurt forever, I swear."

"Yeah, where have I heard that before?" says Jazz, looking straight at me.

"What?" I say.

Ches looks at his sister's feet in amazement. When she spreads her toes, the extra skin between them fans out, just like Layla's does when she submerges in saltwater.

"Jazz, that is some crazy sh—" he starts to say, but his grandmother silences him with a sharp look.

"Damn, Jazz," says Match. "That is so cool. I can't believe my little sister is actually identified. Don't tell me you're going to let that go to waste."

"Easy for you to say," says Jazz. "You didn't just stick your feet in an electric socket."

"Don't be so dramatic," says Match. "It can't possibly hurt any more than one of my burns."

"This from the one who wouldn't step foot in the pool," grumbles Jazz.

The rest of the party turns into an emergency planning session for Jazz's future, bringing my time in the birthday spotlight to an abrupt end. What's new, right? As a middle child, with a swim-star older sister and two attention-seeking younger stepbrothers, I should be used to that by now. Oh, well. I guess half a day as the center of attention is better than nothing.

The plan for Jazz, whether she likes it or not, is to get her examined by a doctor as soon as possible, and then, assuming she's cleared to submerge, to register her for Water school in the fall. But where? As delicately as he can, my dad points out that the public Water school in the Meadow really doesn't have adequate facilities. Jazz's grandmother agrees with that, but what other option is there? Jazz could still attend Fluidity School on scholarship, but because Fluidity is geared toward unidentified teens, it doesn't have any advanced instruction for Waters, or any other source group for that matter.

"What about DWS?" asks Layla, referring to Darwin Water School, which she has attended for the past two years.

"DWS is a wonderful school," says my dad, "but there's the problem of residency."

My mom and Jackie whisper something to each other, then my mom says to Jazz's grandmother, "Louise, I hope we're not over-stepping here, but Jackie and I would be glad to have Jazz stay with us this fall, to get her settled and registered, until something else can be worked out."

"We couldn't impose on you—"

"She can stay on the third floor with me," offers Layla. "There's plenty of room."

That's news to me. It wasn't long ago Layla was begging my mom and Jackie to let her have the third-floor attic room, so she wouldn't have to share a bedroom with me. I guess being part of the exclusive Water club makes all the difference.

"What do you think, Jazz?" asks her grandmother.

Jazz looks at her grandmother, then at Match, who smiles and nods.

"I think ... I'm going to Water school," she says, and the room explodes into cheers.

Well, the more the merrier, I guess, although I'm not really sure Jazz knows what she's getting herself into. This place is a madhouse.

As if to illustrate my point, Devon and Matty come streaking through the living room, each wielding a brightly-colored styrofoam pool noodle, which—I gather from their sound effects—they are using as light sabers.

"Boys," Jackie yells, "take it outside, please."

Ignoring her completely, they run through the kitchen and up the back stairs.

Well, at least some things never change.

ABOUT THE AUTHOR

Jessica V. Barnett works as an attorney in the Boston, Massachusetts area, where she lives with her two sons. This is her first novel.

54374416R00135

Made in the USA
San Bernardino, CA
15 October 2017